PONY CLUB
SECRETS

❧Angel❧

and the
Flying Stallions

The Pony Club Secrets series:

PONY CLUB
SECRETS

Angel
and the
Flying Stallions

Stacy Gregg

HarperCollins *Children's Books*

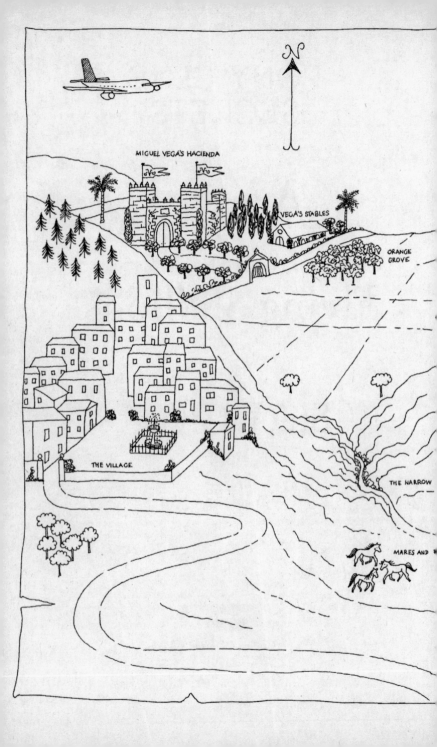

N

MIGUEL VEGA'S HACIENDA

VEGA'S STABLES

ORANGE GROVE

THE VILLAGE

THE NARROW

MARES AND

This book is dedicated to my super agent
Nancy Miles and to her gorgeous horses
Beamish and Apache

www.stacygregg.co.uk

First published in Great Britain by HarperCollins *Children's Books* in 2010
HarperCollins *Children's Books* is a division of HarperCollins*Publishers* Ltd,
1 London Bridge Street, London SE1 9GF.

1

Text copyright © Stacy Gregg 2010
Illustrations © Fiona Land 2009

ISBN 978-0-00-729930-0

Stacy Gregg asserts the moral right to be identified as the author of the work.

Typeset in AGaramond by Palimpsest Book Production Limited,
Falkirk, Stirlingshire

Printed and bound in Great Britain

MIX
Paper from
responsible sources
FSC **FSC™ C007454**
www.fsc.org

CHAPTER 1

It was after midnight in the stables of El Caballo Danza Magnifico, but the bay stallion was wide awake. He paced restlessly in his loose box, his noble head held high as he caught the scent on the night air, nostrils flared and muzzle quivering.

He was not like the other stallions here in Southern Spain. The Lipizzaners and Andalusians in these stables boasted famous bloodlines that could be traced back for centuries. Valuable beyond measure, each of the stallions had been schooled in the ways of classical dressage, trained to perform the elaborate manoeuvres of the *haute école*.

The bay stallion was leaner and more streamlined

than the stocky Spanish purebreds in the stalls around him. His Andalusian blood had been mixed with Arabian and Thoroughbred, which imbued him with a rare speed and stamina that the heavy-set purebreds could never possess.

His name was Storm, and when he had first arrived at El Caballo he had been no more than a leggy and headstrong young colt. Since then he had grown strong, grazing with the herd on the upper pastures in the shadow of the mountains of the Sierra de Grazalema. The colt had become a stallion, and at sixteen-three hands high he was even taller than his sire, the great grey stallion Marius, who was currently asleep in his loose box just a few doors along.

In the still of the night, Storm could hear the sound of hoofbeats approaching at a gallop. He raised his elegant head into the air and let loose a whinny. His sharp call was a warning cry to the herd of mares grazing the pastures outside the walls of the compound. Danger was coming.

The mares heard the bay stallion's clarion call and a moment later they too heard the thunder of hooves drawing closer.

The herd was gripped with panic and the mares and their foals began to scatter in every direction. One of the mares, Margarita, a pale grey beauty with coal-black eyes, immediately took charge of the situation. She was the alpha mare – the leader of the herd – and the others would follow her command. She acted quickly, nipping and kicking at the mares to make them do her bidding, rounding them up to move away from the approaching threat. Many of the mares had young foals at foot slowing them down, but Margarita urged them to be quick, attacking stragglers with squeals and bites, keeping the group tight so that no foal or mare would be left behind. Within seconds they were grouped together, ready to run – but where to? The gates to the hacienda had been closed for the evening so they could not come in to the safety of the courtyard.

The mares began to circle helplessly, driven into a frenzy, as Margarita fought to keep the herd together. If any foal or mare broke away now and left the safety of the herd they would be in even greater danger!

Inside the stables, Storm sensed that the galloping horses were very near now, but he could do nothing to help the mares. In desperation, he rose up on his hind legs and brought his front hooves crashing down hard on the door of his stall. But the doors were made of solid oak, built to withstand a thousand strikes, and his hooves barely scratched their surface. Frustrated and helpless, the bay stallion held his head high and whinnied again. This time the piercing urgency in his cry carried through the night and reached not only the mares, but the sleeping occupants of the hacienda.

Inside the house, lights flickered on. There were shouts of confusion and a moment later three figures came out on to the front step – Roberto Nunez, the owner of El Caballo Danza Magnifico, his son Alfonso, and his head dressage trainer Francoise D'arth. All three were still in their pyjamas and they hurriedly pulled on riding boots and raced down the steps into the cobbled courtyard.

"Go and check on the stallions' stables," Roberto instructed Francoise. "Alfonso, put on the floodlights in the courtyard and open the gates. I'll bring in the mares!"

As Alfonso and Francoise set off running across the courtyard, Roberto turned around and ran back inside the hacienda. When he re-emerged a moment later, he had a shotgun in his hands. If his mares were being attacked by wolves or rounded up by bandits then he needed to be fully prepared.

As soon as Alfonso switched on the courtyard lights and heaved open the heavy wrought iron gates the terrified herd of mares swung about at full gallop and headed for the safety of the compound.

There was a mad clatter as the mares' hooves struck the cobbled stone of the courtyard and they galloped in to safety, their foals running alongside them.

"Are any mares missing?" Alfonso asked his father.

There were over twenty mares gathered in the middle of the courtyard. To anyone else they would have appeared almost identical, and yet Roberto Nunez could tell them apart at a glance. His eyes flitted swiftly across the herd and he breathed a sigh of relief. All of his prized mares and their offspring were here and they were safe!

"Close the gates!" Roberto ordered. Alfonso pushed the heavy gates shut once more and then came over to join his father. "We'll have to start bringing the mares in again at night," he told Roberto. "I think there are wolves about."

"No," Roberto Nunez shook his head. "Something was out there tonight, but I don't think it was wolves."

"Bandits? Vega's men maybe?" Alfonso asked.

"Perhaps." Roberto looked uncertain. "The question is, did they intend to steal the mares or were they after an even greater prize?"

As he said this, Francoise D'arth emerged from the stallions' stable block and ran towards them. Although she was French, and not Spanish like Roberto and his son, she could easily have been mistaken for a member of the family with her long black hair and lithe lean physique, earned through long hours in the saddle.

"I've checked the stalls," she told Roberto Nunez. "The stallions are safe."

"All of them?" Roberto asked nervously. "Even the Little One?"

Despite the fact that Storm was actually the tallest stallion in his stables, Roberto could not break the habit of referring to him by his nickname – Little One.

Francoise smiled. "Nightstorm is fine. He must have been the one that sensed the danger. I am certain that it was his call that woke me."

"Well," Roberto said, "we take no more chances. From now on the mares must be brought in again each night."

He looked at Francoise. "Perhaps you should assign

one of your grooms to stand guard by the stallions' stables for the next few nights as well."

"*Oui*," Francoise agreed with him, "I'll organise a roster. Meanwhile, I will stay with the horses tonight."

Roberto seemed satisfied with this plan. "Keep a close eye on the Little One," he told her.

"Of course I will," Francoise nodded. She knew how important Storm was. Nothing must happen to the young stallion, especially now. In two days' time, his mistress was arriving in Spain to claim him.

Far away on the other side of the world, in Chevalier Point, Storm's owner, Issie Brown, was utterly unaware of the danger her horse was in. All her thoughts were focused on just one thing – getting a clear round.

The showjumping fences in front of Issie were set at a metre-twenty and it was a tough course. Thankfully Comet, the skewbald gelding she was riding, could eat jumps like these for breakfast.

A clear round was vital if they wanted to win today at the Chevalier Point one-day event.

A combined score from all three phases – dressage, cross country and showjumping – would decide the winner. Issie and Comet's weakness in the dressage phase that morning meant they went into the cross country with a decidedly average score.

Issie wasn't surprised – dressage was never their forte. Instead, the partnership relied on blitzing their competition on the cross country and showjumping courses to pull them up the rankings. So far they'd managed to go clear and fast around a tricky cross-country course that had got the better of many of the other riders. Providing Issie could coax Comet to yet another clear round in the showjumping phase, they had every chance of winning a ribbon.

Even though Comet was a bold cross-country ride, he was also a remarkably careful showjumper. He hardly ever scraped the rails, picking up his feet cleanly over the jumps. As they set off around the course, the skewbald felt fresh and eager despite his exertions across country just a few hours earlier. He took the first three fences with deceptive ease, jumping them as if they were no more than trotting poles. At the treble Issie tried to check the skewbald in preparation for the jump, but Comet gave an indignant snort as if to say, "Leave me alone, I know what I'm doing!" He shook his head defiantly to loosen the reins and bounded forward in a bouncy canter, popping the first fence on a perfect canter stride and then leaping to take all three fences without so much as grazing a pole!

"Good boy!" Issie gave the skewbald a slappy pat on his sweaty neck and turned him towards the spread. They took it neatly and cantered on. Only two more jumps and they would be done. The skewbald pony was now hitting his stride and he cantered towards the next fence with ears pricked forward. Issie turned Comet sharply in mid-air over the jump and by the time they landed they already had the next fence in their sights. It was a wide oxer, and as they flew it with a huge leap the crowd broke into spontaneous applause. Only one more jump to go! At the final fence Comet stood back and jumped far too wide. This time his hooves scraped across the top rail, rocking it in its metal cups and there was a horrified gasp from the crowd. It was Issie's turn now to hold her breath as she waited to hear the pole fall. She was beyond relieved when she heard the audience give a whoop and break into applause once again. The pole hadn't fallen! Clear round!

As he raced through the finish flags, Comet saluted his victory with a gleeful buck, and Issie had to grab a hank of mane to stay onboard. She was still grinning when Tom Avery, her instructor, met her at the arena gates.

"If I didn't know better," Issie said as she slid down from the skewbald's back, "I would say Comet scraped that last rail on purpose, just to give the crowd a bit of drama."

Avery laughed. "You know, I was thinking the same thing."

He took Comet's reins so that Issie could undo her helmet. Comet, as usual, was refusing to stand still. He wanted to go back into the arena and show off in front of the crowds again!

"You'll get your chance in a moment," Issie told the pony. "We'll have to go in for the prize-giving. That clear round has raised us up to third place!"

The skewbald gelding had his head held high and was looking around, as if waiting for more applause for his antics. Issie gave him a pat on his patchy chestnut and white neck. "He's going to miss all of the attention once he's turned out."

Avery nodded. "Comet's certainly earned the break this season." He smiled at Issie. "As have you."

Six months ago Issie had turned up on Tom Avery's doorstep with a serious proposal. She told him that she wanted to become an international eventing rider – and she wanted Avery to become her trainer.

Avery had warned Issie that working her way to the top of the international circuit would be a huge commitment. He told her that there would be a gruelling physical training schedule and that a professional rider needed more than just talent. They must have absolute, unwavering dedication.

Issie replied that she understood – she was totally committed to her goal. This was all Avery needed to hear. Ever since then he had taken up the challenge without hesitation and, even though he had his hands full with both Dulmoth Park and the pony club to run, he was totally focused on turning Issie's dream of international eventing into a reality.

"The first thing we need to do is get you a horse," Avery had told her that day. With his new position as head of the Dulmoth Park stables, Avery could offer her the pick of the best eventing hacks.

"You can have any one you like," Avery told Issie, "but if I were you, I would stick with Comet."

Issie was shocked. Comet was a Blackthorn Pony, born and bred on her Aunt Hester's farm. Issie adored him and had been very successful in the showjumping ring with him, but she couldn't believe Avery rated the fourteen-two pony above the fancy sporthorses at Dulmoth Park.

"Don't judge him by his size or his bloodlines," Avery told her. "Comet has proven himself a brilliant showjumper. He picks his feet up more carefully over the jumps than any horse I've ever met. And he's bold and fearless, so he'll make a great cross-country horse."

The only problem that Avery could see was Comet's dressage. "He's too hot-headed," Avery admitted. "He lacks the patience for dressage…" adding with a smile, "… and, to be honest, you're not much better, Issie!"

She took the criticism good-naturedly. After all, her instructor had a point. Issie couldn't deny that she found dressage schooling sessions dull. She would always find an excuse to skip the flatwork and take Comet out jumping instead. Comet was just as bad, if not worse. The skewbald pony made it clear that he loathed trotting around the dressage arena and would act nappy and behave sluggishly. In the end, Issie would give up and they would tear off to do some cross-country jumps instead.

As a consequence, their first season together on the eventing circuit had been a series of appalling dressage tests followed by spotless clear rounds in both cross country and showjumping. Sometimes this was enough to elevate the duo in the final rankings and they would still manage to win a rosette, but Avery was still very hard on Issie about her lack of commitment to resolve her dressage schooling issues. He had pointed out to her that several times this season they had been pushed down the rankings and had ended up out of the prize money because their flatwork simply wasn't up to scratch.

Despite the skewbald pony's disdain for dressage, Issie knew that Avery considered him a serious eventing prospect for the future. But Comet's future would have to wait. The eventing season in New Zealand was over for another year and Avery had decided that Comet should be spelled – turned out and left unridden for a month – to recuperate before the new season began in spring.

As the worst of winter set in, Comet would be having

a horsey holiday with his paddock mates, Toby and Marmite, down at the River Paddock. Issie's two best friends, Stella and Kate, were keeping an eye on the horses for the next few weeks. Issie, meanwhile, was about to set off to collect the horse that Avery pinned so much hope on for her international eventing career.

When Issie had told Avery her dream, he knew that she needed the right horse to take her to the top. Comet was on the list of potential mounts. But there was also another horse that Avery had in mind. Not just any horse, but *the* horse. If Avery was correct, this stallion would be talented enough to take Issie to the highest level, competing in international, four star events. A horse like this would normally cost a fortune but, luckily for Issie, she already owned the perfect horse. And right now he was waiting for her, far away in Southern Spain.

Issie's bags were packed and the plane tickets were ready. Tomorrow they would board the plane to travel once again to El Caballo Danza Magnifico. There, she would be reunited with her beloved Nightstorm. And this time, they wouldn't be separated again. This time, she was bringing him home.

CHAPTER 2

Issie's last flight to Spain had been one of the worst times of her life. Nightstorm had been stolen from Chevalier Point and Issie had gone after him, spending the entire twenty-four-hour journey worried sick that she might never see her colt again. This time, however, the butterflies in her tummy as she boarded the plane to Madrid were not from fear, but from excitement.

It had been a difficult decision, when she chose to leave Storm behind at El Caballo Danza Magnifico all those months ago. She knew deep down that she had done the right thing, but that hadn't made it any easier. She still remembered how it broke her heart to hug Storm goodbye.

When she said goodbye to him, Storm had still been a leggy yearling. Now, by all accounts, he was fully grown – a strapping stallion! Issie was beside herself with excitement at the prospect of being reunited with her horse. It was almost impossible to sit still on the plane. Her nervous energy didn't escape the attention of the passenger sat to her left.

"Are you going to keep jiggling about like that for the whole trip?" Mrs Brown asked as Issie squirmed in the cramped economy-class seat beside her. She peered over at her daughter's tray table. "Look! You've barely touched your food."

"Mum," Issie groaned, "it's airline food! No one touches it."

"Do you want me to ask the cabin crew if they have something else?" Mrs Brown asked.

"No, Mum," Issie smiled. "Stop fussing over me. I'm fine."

It had come as a bit of a shock to Issie that her mum would be accompanying her and Avery on the journey to El Caballo Danza Magnifico.

"I don't see why you're so surprised," Mrs Brown had said. "I need to keep an eye on you after last time.

I don't want you entering another Spanish horse race!"

Issie's mother was still upset about her last trip there. "Racing horses through the streets!" Mrs Brown shook her head. "What were you thinking?"

If Mrs Brown had actually seen how Issie had ridden the El Caballo stallion, Angel, that day then she would have had a heart attack! The Silver Bridle was a wild, winner-takes-all contest, run through the town square of the local village. Issie had galloped against hardened, Spanish *vaqueros* – cowboys twice her size who rode with ruthless determination.

"I had no choice," Issie had shrugged in her defence. "It was the only way to get Storm back from Miguel Vega."

Issie had won the race and the colt had been returned to her safe and sound. She had been intent on bringing Storm back home immediately, but Roberto Nunez persuaded her not to. He convinced Issie to leave Storm with him in Spain at El Caballo Danza Magnifico so that the colt could receive an education in the art of *haute école* – the 'high school' dressage movements.

"I still don't understand why you want to come, Mum," Issie had said when her mother told her of her plans. "We're not going to some seaside resort on the Costa Del Sol! This is a horse farm in the middle of nowhere. You don't even like horses!"

"I'm coming because I need to keep an eye on you!" Mrs Brown said. "Besides, I've always wanted to go on holiday to Southern Spain. And the weather is perfect in Andalusia right now."

Issie couldn't argue with that. July was mid-summer in Spain, a pleasant change from Chevalier Point, where the nastiest month of winter was about to set in. They would be leaving behind rain, mud and chilly mornings in favour of thirty degree temperatures, sunshine and blue skies for five whole weeks! It seemed like a long time just to collect a horse, but Avery had insisted that they needed to stay for at least a month to "do the training work and fulfil the terms of the contract with Francoise" – whatever that meant.

Avery had been vague about the details, but then he seemed rather preoccupied lately. Issie guessed that he had a lot on his mind; organising this trip back to El Caballo, emailing and phoning Francoise regularly to discuss their plans.

It had taken a whole six months to negotiate the

arrangements for bringing Storm home. Francoise, in her capacity as head trainer at El Caballo Danza Magnifico, had resisted the idea at first. She felt the stallion needed more time to continue his training and she had been reluctant to let Storm go. Eventually, however, she and Avery had reached an agreement and a date was set for Issie, her mum and her trainer to travel to Spain.

It wasn't a simple journey to undertake. The flight to Spain from New Zealand took twenty-four hours and after that there was a high-speed train from Madrid to Seville. By the time the three travellers arrived at the railway station in Seville they were jetlagged and exhausted. The heat of the sun struck Issie as she wheeled her suitcase out of the front doors. It was so intense that she felt like she was melting into the pavement. She cast a glance at the road ahead and suddenly caught sight of the familiar beaten-up old Land Rover parked directly in front of the train station. There was a lanky teenager leaning back against the bonnet of the car. He had tousled black hair, tanned skin and the square-jawed good looks of a Spanish film star. The boy waved to Issie and his face broke into a broad grin.

"Alfie!" Issie squealed as she dropped her luggage and made a dash across the busy street, throwing herself into his arms.

Mrs Brown watched wide-eyed as her daughter hugged him. "The local Spanish lads are very friendly with tourists, aren't they?" she commented dryly to Avery as they followed across the road with the luggage.

"Mum!" Issie was beaming. "This is Alfonso Nunez. He's the son of Roberto and the head rider in El Caballo Danza Magnifico."

"Lovely to meet you, Mrs Brown," Alfie said, letting go of Issie and racing forward to help with the luggage. "We're very excited that you could join your daughter on this trip," he smiled. "Isadora has told me how much you love horses and what a great rider you are. My father has already chosen one of his most spirited stallions and asked one of the men to prepare him for you to ride. We can saddle up as soon as we get to the hacienda!"

Mrs Brown's face dropped. "Ride?" She turned to Issie in panic. "He is joking, isn't he, Isadora? You did tell him that I'm utterly terrified of horses, didn't you?"

Alfie and Issie couldn't keep straight faces any longer and burst out laughing.

"Very funny!" Mrs Brown fumed as she clambered into the back seat of the Land Rover. Alfie and Avery loaded the last of the bags, then Alfie leapt into the driver's seat and turned the Land Rover out on to the cobbled streets of downtown Seville.

Within an hour they had left the city and begun to climb through the forest-clad hills of Andalusia. As Alfie turned off the main road, yellow dust flew up from beneath the tyres and he began to steer more vigorously to avoid the potholes in the rugged road that wound around the hills. Soon they were surrounded by olive trees and then as the Land Rover began to descend into a green valley Issie felt her heart soar. There it was, El Caballo Danza Magnifico! Down below she could see the herds of mares with their foals grazing the sunburnt fields around the perimeter of the estate, its beautiful stone buildings arranged around a cobbled courtyard and enclosed by a vast, white stone wall.

"The mares are only allowed out to graze during the daytime now," Alfie told Issie as they drove down the hill. "There was an incident last week, late at night. We think maybe it was bandits trying to raid the herd."

Issie was horrified. "The mares and foals were all fine,"

Alfie reassured her, "but since then Dad has insisted that we bring the horses in every night, just to be safe."

"Do you think it might have been Miguel Vega's men?" Issie asked.

Miguel Vega's hacienda was El Caballo's closest neighbour. The two great horse farms had been fierce rivals for many years and Vega was not above resorting to dirty tricks.

"Miguel Vega?" Mrs Brown joined in the conversation. "Why do I know that name?"

"He's the one that stole Storm," Issie reminded her mother.

Alfonso nodded. "Since your last visit, *Señor* Vega has been suspiciously quiet. I wondered how long it would be before he gave us trouble again." Alfie shrugged. "Whoever it was, we have taken precautions now. The mares are locked up at night. It will not be easy for them to try again."

The herd was grazing near the dusty road as they drove past and even Mrs Brown was captured by the beauty of these mares with their charcoal-black foals. "Why are the mothers white when their foals are black?" she asked.

"Lipizzaners and Andalusians are grey, but their foals

are always born black," Avery explained. "Their coats change colour as they age. Eventually the dark colour fades away completely and the horses become grey."

"They don't look grey," Mrs Brown said stubbornly. "They're white really, aren't they?"

Issie sighed. Her mum was the most unhorsey person she knew. "Mum, technically there's no such thing as a white horse," Issie explained. "They're always called grey."

"We have over fifty horses," Alfie told Mrs Brown, taking up the role as El Caballo tour guide. "All of them are bred here. We have the Lipizzaners and Andalusians, and we also have Anglo-Arabs – the same bloodlines as Isadora's own mare, Blaze."

Alfie pulled the Land Rover to a rough stop outside the gates of the hacienda and Issie leapt out of the car, swung open the enormous wrought iron gates and let him through. Alfie drove sedately around the cobbled compound, continuing his tour for the benefit of Mrs Brown. "That large building to the rear is the mares' quarters, where we keep them at night," he explained. "The stallions are in separate quarters over there and that building ahead of you now is our main indoor arena where the riders train the horses. And this…" he said, swinging hard on the wheel of the Land Rover, turning back around the fountain and parking the car in front of the central archway of the main hacienda, "… is our house, where you will be staying as our guests."

Mrs Brown was stunned. "Much nicer than the Costa Del Sol!" she muttered.

The Nunez hacienda was a stately Spanish villa, two storeys high with curved archways on the bottom floor and top-floor balconies smothered in vines of brilliant pink and orange tropical bougainvillea. All the windows were trimmed with wrought iron window boxes filled with candy pink geraniums, and the front steps were lined with elegant topiaries of Seville oranges. The front door was made of heavy, dark-stained wood. It swung open and a man stepped out to greet them.

"Thomas!" Roberto Nunez skipped down the stairs and grasped Avery by the hand before pulling him into his arms in a manly embrace. "So good to see you again!"

"You too, Roberto," Avery hugged the Spaniard who had been his best friend ever since they met as young riders on the international eventing circuit.

"And Isadora!" Roberto smiled. "Welcome back. And this lovely woman must be your sister?"

He stepped forward, took Mrs Brown's hand and clasped it lightly in his own.

"Roberto," said Issie, grinning at his charming antics, "this is my mum, Amanda Brown."

"Welcome!" Roberto smiled. "Don't worry about your luggage. Alfonso will take it to your rooms. Come in and sit down! Have something to eat and drink. You must be famished."

He guided his guests towards the front door of the hacienda.

"Where is Francoise?" Avery asked, looking around.

"Down at the stallions' stables," Roberto replied. "Isadora, perhaps you might like to go and let her know you have arrived?"

Issie's heart was racing as she headed across the cobbled courtyard. It was so strange to be back here again! She couldn't believe she was about to see Storm. Her stomach was tied in nervous knots. It had been so long.

The stallions' quarters were located on the far side of the compound. From the outside they looked like all the rest of the buildings at El Caballo Danza Magnifico; classical Spanish stone with curved archways and tiled rooftops. But inside was a different story. The stallions' quarters were ultra-modern and the loose boxes were state-of-the-art.

Issie looked down the row of stalls and at the far end of the corridor she saw Francoise D'arth. The French dressage trainer was wearing cream jodhpurs and a white shirt, her long dark hair tied back in a high ponytail. She was leading a horse and with one glimpse of the pretty, dished Arabian face with the wide, white blaze Issie knew it was him.

"Storm!" she called out, unable to control her excitement.

The horse suddenly froze at the sound of her voice and stood alert with his head held high. Without thinking, Issie raised a hand to her lips and gave a wolf whistle – the call she had always used back home when she played tag with the colt.

At the sound of the whistle, Storm let out a loud nicker and began to dance and skip, going up on to his hind legs so that Francoise was forced to pull him back down.

"Storm! Easy boy, no!" Issie cried out, aware that her call had rattled the big bay stallion.

It was too late. Storm reared up a second time with such force that he ripped the lead rope out of Francoise's hands.

Francoise was an experienced horsewoman, but she hadn't been expecting this and the stallion was too powerful. He broke free from her hands and surged forward, heading straight for the girl. His metal horseshoes chimed out against the hard concrete floor beneath his hooves as he cantered through the stable block.

Issie stood perfectly still. The bay stallion's enormous, muscled body was thundering through the stables. She knew that he could easily trample her down or knock her over, and yet, as the horse continued to bear down on her, Issie wasn't in the least bit afraid. This wasn't any stallion, this was her horse. It was Storm.

The girl and the stallion were just a few metres apart when Storm pulled up dramatically to a halt and stood, snorting and quivering, in front of her. The stallion was sixteen-three hands high and every inch of him was pure muscle. Issie looked into his deep brown eyes and didn't hesitate. She threw herself forward and flung her arms around the horse's neck, burying her face in his long, black mane.

"Storm!" Issie was finding it hard to breathe, a sob was stuck in her throat and she was choking on her words. "Hey boy, it's me."

The stallion was trembling all over, nickering and stamping, flicking his head as if to say, "You're back! Where have you been all this time? I missed you!"

At the far end of the corridor, Francoise D'arth watched this touching reunion and a faint smile crossed her lips. She had never seen a horse behave like that before, but then she had never known any horse and rider to have a bond as close as the one Issie shared with Storm. The girl loved the bay stallion and he had missed her dreadfully. But as Francoise knew only too well, it was not enough to love a horse. You must also have the skills to handle it. In the month to come, Issie would need to prove herself at El Caballo Danza Magnifico. But for now, Francoise stood back and let Isadora enjoy the reunion with her beloved horse. The girl would find out soon enough about the nature of the challenge that lay ahead.

CHAPTER 3

When Storm was nothing more than a skinny-legged colt running around the paddocks at Winterflood Farm, Issie had trained him to come when she whistled. It was a cute trick to teach a foal, but it was a totally different story now he had become a fully-grown stallion.

"I'm sorry," Issie called out to Francoise as she led Storm back up the corridor, "I can't believe he still remembers my whistle."

"It is my fault," Francoise replied as she strode forward to meet them. "I should have anticipated his reaction. They say that horses do not remember as you and I do, but this is not always true. Some memories run so deep they cannot be erased. He has not forgotten you, Isadora.

That is quite clear."

As if to confirm this, Storm gave another nicker and rubbed his handsome face up against Issie, using her as a scratching post just as he had always done in the padddock back home.

"Storm!" Francoise chastised the stallion. "Where are your manners? An El Caballo stallion doesn't behave like that!"

Francoise took the lead rope and jiggled it to make him step back. Storm got the message and stood obediently while Francoise embraced Issie in the customary French way with a kiss on each cheek before adding a hug of her own.

"Welcome back to El Caballo Danza Magnifico, Isadora," she smiled.

"It's good to be back, Francoise," Issie grinned.

Issie had been hoping that perhaps they could saddle up straight away. She was desperate to ride Storm for the first time and Francoise seemed to be reading her mind. "There will be time for riding soon enough," the Frenchwoman said as she grasped Storm's lead rope and began to guide him down the corridor back towards his stall, "I don't think Roberto would be impressed if I took his guest out for a gallop straight away. We should go back into the house and get you settled in." She smiled at Issie. "That is, if you can possibly bear to be apart from Storm again!"

Issie laughed at this, but really she would rather have stayed out here, exhausted, grubby and jetlagged, and fallen asleep beside her horse on the straw in his stall than go to the luxury and comfort of her room in the Nunez hacienda. But Issie knew that would have sounded ungrateful, so she followed Francoise as she led the stallion back to his loose box.

"He has grown up so beautifully, hasn't he? Look at his topline!" Francoise gestured at the ridge of muscle along the stallion's neck just beneath the glossy, black mane. "You can see by the developing muscles that we have already begun his training in the dressage school. He is still too young for the advanced *haute école* manoeuvres. They will come later. We are taking things gradually, but already my riders think he shows great promise. Once he learns collection and paces he will be ready to progress to the 'airs above ground'."

Issie felt herself tense up. Francoise was talking about Storm as if he still had more training to come. But how could that be possible when they were here to take him home to Chevalier Point? Francoise was acting as if he wasn't actually going to leave El Caballo Danza Magnifico!

"We'll keep training him when we get him home, of course," Issie said, hoping that she was subtly making it clear that she expected to take the colt back with her, "but dressage isn't really my priority. Avery believes Storm will be a great prospect as an eventer."

Francoise looked serious. "We have had long discussions about this, Tom and I. When you first agreed to keep the colt with us, it was so that he could be schooled as a classical dressage horse. And, as I have been trying to impress upon Tom, his training has not yet finished."

"What do you mean, he hasn't finished?" Issie was getting edgy. "I'm here to take him home."

Francoise frowned. "But surely you know about this? I made it clear to Avery that I could not permit you to take Storm away now. The stallion's basic training has begun, but he has yet to learn the truly advanced moves of dressage. It would be wrong to drag him out of the best classical school in the world when you could not possibly complete his training back home in Chevalier

Point. Only an *haute école* rider will do for a horse such as Storm. That is why we came to the arrangement."

Issie was taken aback. "Arrangement? What arrangement?" This couldn't be happening! "I've come all this way and now you're telling me I can't take my own horse home?"

"*Non, non!*" Francoise shook her head. "That is not what I am saying. Of course you will take him." She paused. "But first, you must fulfil your side of bargain. That was the deal that I struck with Tom."

The conversation had grown tense. Issie desperately wanted to make a childish snatch and take back the stallion's lead rope. She was jetlagged and on the verge of tears, trying to behave like an adult. But Issie didn't feel very grown-up. She didn't want to be having this conversation. She just wanted her horse.

Footsteps echoed in the stable block, and Francoise and Issie both turned to see Avery walking up the corridor to join them.

Francoise emphatically slid the bolt on the door, as if to make a point that the stallion was still under El Caballo lock and key, and then turned to face Avery with her hands on her hips. "I assumed you would have explained it to her by now. What is going on here?"

Francoise's abruptness took Avery by surprise. "Well, bonjour to you too!" he smiled at her. "I was expecting at least a French kiss on the cheek before we started fighting."

His amused expression seemed to infuriate Francoise. "Do not be cute with me! We made a contract. And, since it involves Isadora too, I thought you would have told her about it."

Avery's smile disappeared. "I did tell her. I said that we would be staying here for at least a month to fulfil the terms of the training contract."

Francoise shook her head as if she was trying to rearrange jigsaw-puzzle pieces inside her brain. "But you didn't tell her anything more than that?"

"Hey!" Issie was getting fed up with the to-and-fro between Avery and Francoise. "I'm standing right here! Will you please stop bickering and tell me what's going on?"

Francoise cast a sullen look at Avery then turned to Issie. "If you want to take Storm home to Chevalier Point, you must know how to train him first."

"I know how to train a horse," Issie frowned. "I've

schooled Fortune and Comet. I'm quite capable of teaching Storm the basics…"

"No," Francoise interrupted her, "not the basics, Isadora. If you want to take Storm you must know how to continue his dressage education. You must learn the ways of classical dressage so that you can ride the *haute école*."

Issie was gobsmacked. "You're kidding me, right? Francoise, I can barely get through a dressage test for a one-day event. I can't do any fancy moves!"

"Believe me, Issie," Avery interjected, "Francoise is only too aware of your limitations when it comes to dressage."

"Tom has told me about your riding on the eventing circuit," Francoise continued. "Your dressage tests are, without fail, sub-standard. This is why I insisted that you must stay and learn *haute école*."

"You agreed to this?" Issie was stunned. "It's like you're checking me into some kind of dressage rehab! You're both ganging up on me!"

"It's not like that," Avery said. "You might not realise it now, but you will benefit enormously from what Francoise is suggesting."

"You will have a month at El Caballo training in the

dressage school with my riders," Francoise explained. "The performers are all in training mode preparing their new routines for the upcoming touring season, so the timing couldn't be better. You will train with the school as if you were one of them. It is a great honour, as I am sure you can appreciate. These riders are some of the best horsemen in the world. Their knowledge of dressage is second to none."

Francoise was right. Her riders were amazing. The manoeuvres they could perform on their horses were nothing short of astonishing to watch. But Issie had never imagined herself in the same league. She wasn't capable of performing this intricate ballet on horseback. She would only embarrass herself in front of Francoise's riders. It sounded like a nightmare to Issie, but her fate had been sealed before she even set foot on Spanish soil. Avery and Francoise had agreed to this. She had to learn the *haute école* or she would not be allowed to take Storm home with her. She did not doubt that Francoise was quite serious about this. Or that Avery had agreed to it. She knew that neither of these formidable trainers would take no for an answer.

"OK, but I don't understand how I'm going to do

this," Issie frowned. "You said a minute ago that Storm was still too young to learn *haute école*."

"He is," Francoise confirmed. "You will not be riding Storm in the school. You will be riding another horse."

Francoise turned on her heels and led Issie and Avery further down the corridor of the stallions' stables until they reached the stall at the end. Here she swung open the top of the Dutch door to reveal the horse that stood inside.

The stallion was almost as tall as Storm, sixteen-two hands high. His face had the noble bearing of a classical Andalusian with wide-set, soulful eyes and a dark, sooty muzzle. He was a grey, but his dapples had long ago faded so he was as creamy white as parchment. His long mane was like gossamer silk and it tumbled and cascaded over his broad neck and down his powerful shoulders. Only one thing marred this stallion's pure and exquisite beauty – on the bridge of his Roman nose, just where the noseband of a bridle rests, were tiny jagged scars where once there had been deep cuts in the stallion's flesh. The wounds were very old now and had healed over with time. Issie knew exactly how the stallion had received these scars – from wearing a cruel *serreta* bridle in the hands of Miguel Vega.

She reached up and stroked the stallion's soft muzzle, touching the scar tissue tenderly as she looked deep into his dark, liquid eyes.

"Hello, Angel," she said softly to him. "It's me. I've come back."

CHAPTER 4

Mrs Brown was astonished when Issie told her that dinner at El Caballo Danza Magnifico was at 10 p.m.

"But that's the time I usually go to bed!"

"They do things differently here in Spain," Issie told her. "There's an afternoon siesta and then we eat dinner late."

The Spanish afternoon siesta was the perfect way to sleep off their jetlag. Issie had been given the same room as last time, on the second floor with its own balcony overlooking the cobbled courtyard. Like the rest of the house, the room had dark-polished wood floors strewn with colourful, Moorish rugs. The walls of the bedroom were rustic plaster, tinted deep pink, and hung with ornate mirrors. Issie had flopped down on the rainbow-striped bedspread and fallen straight to sleep. When she woke up she was utterly starving and it was nearly 10 p.m.

Downstairs the massive dining table was decorated with vases of orange roses and was heaving with food. There was 'rich man's paella' made with squid and spicy sausage, served with tomato bread, olives, and a huge plate of fried calamari and salt cod. To drink there was orange juice from the El Caballo's orchard and red wine. Roberto poured them each a drink, then raised his own glass aloft.

"I would like to welcome back old friends," he said, then smiled at Mrs Brown, "and new ones as well."

Mrs Brown had helped Roberto to prepare the dinner that evening, and their vigorous discussions of Spanish food had prompted Roberto to mention the *feria* – the country fair that was being held in the village that weekend. The *feria* was a big event for the district, with food and dancing and, of course, all the local horse breeders with their best mares and stallions on display.

"It sounds amazing!" Mrs Brown enthused. "I'd love to go!"

Roberto smiled. "Excellent. We will all ride there

together. I have a beautiful stallion, Ferdinand. He is so docile and kind he will be the perfect horse for you to ride. I shall make sure the stable hands prepare him for you."

"All right," Mrs Brown said nervously.

Issie gave a gasp and nearly choked on a mouthful of paella.

"What? Mum, you're going to ride?"

"Isadora," her mum laughed, "I'm sure if Roberto says the horse is suitable for me then I'll be fine."

Issie couldn't believe it. Neither could Alfie, who was sitting beside her. "I thought your mother was terrified of horses?" he whispered to Issie.

"She is!" Issie whispered back.

"It's nice for Dad to have company his own age," Alfie noted. "He's alone quite a lot, while we're away touring with the horses."

Roberto Nunez was a widower. Alfie's mum had died when he was only six and Roberto had never remarried. Roberto was a bit like her mum, Issie thought. Mrs Brown had split up with Issie's dad when Issie was nine and she had been on her own ever since, bringing up Issie single-handedly.

Issie only wished that Francoise and Avery were getting along as well as her mum and Roberto seemed to be. The trainers spent most of the dinner bickering about the smallest, inconsequential things. It had started when Avery had commented on how nice Francoise's hair looked, swept back off her face and arranged in a twist in the Spanish style, with a large tortoiseshell comb holding it in place.

"So you do not like my hair when it is worn down?" Francoise had countered.

"I never said that," Avery was taken aback. "I only said it looked very nice tonight."

"You know," Francoise said, "I did not put my hair up like this just so I could get comments from you."

"You mean you'd prefer it if I didn't say that your hair looked nice?" Avery was confused.

"Exactly!" Francoise said.

Roberto, meanwhile, had noticed that Issie was not her usual self. "You have been very quiet tonight, Isadora," Roberto noted. "I thought you would be excited about beginning your *haute école* training tomorrow?"

"Umm," Issie didn't know how to answer this. "I guess so."

Roberto frowned. "That does not sound like enthusiasm to me."

Issie picked at her paella with her fork. "I'm not cut out for dressage," she admitted. "I'm more of a cross-country kind of rider, I guess."

"Ah yes, I have heard all about your plans to become an eventer," Roberto nodded sagely. "When I began my riding career as an eventer I too had little regard for the classical art. But once you see the beauty of the *haute école* perhaps you will learn to appreciate it. You will certainly find that the next few months here with us will not be wasted…"

"A few months!" Issie forgot her manners once more. "How long is this going to take?"

"It takes a lifetime to master the *haute école*," Roberto answered.

"I don't have a lifetime. I only have five weeks," Issie said. "I need to get back to Chevalier Point. The new season will be starting and—"

"These things cannot be rushed. You will be able to leave when you are capable of looking after the Little One and know how to train him correctly," Roberto said firmly.

Issie began to protest, casting a pleading look at Avery,

but her complaints were cut short by a hammering at the front door.

"Are we expecting any company?" Roberto asked, looking at Francoise and Alfie. Both of them shook their heads. It was eleven o'clock at night. Even by Spanish standards, it was late for a visitor to be calling.

Roberto stood up from the table and was about to get the door when the banging stopped and footsteps echoed in the hall. The dining-room door suddenly swung open and standing there in front of them was the squat, tubby figure of Miguel Vega.

"What?" Vega demanded. "You do not answer your front door when someone is knocking?"

"You hardly gave me the chance!" Roberto Nunez replied. He was too amused by Vega's sheer cheek to be truly outraged by his neighbour barging in. "What do you want, Miguel?"

Vega didn't answer. His eyes had widened at the sight of Isadora.

"Aha!" he grinned like a hyena. "The chica! The little girl who beat me in the race! I should have known she was behind this!"

"What are you talking about, Vega?" Roberto Nunez

was losing his good humour rapidly. "You storm into my house and…"

"Do not try to blame this on me!" Vega shot back. "You know what you have done, Roberto. No doubt the girl was involved. Well you will not get away with it! Give her back!"

Roberto was baffled. He looked at Isadora.

"No, no!" Vega shook his head. "Not the girl. I don't want her back. I want the mare. The one you stole from me!"

"What?" Roberto was stunned.

"Hand her back now and we will say no more about it," Vega said. There were beads of sweat appearing in the furrows of his brow, glistening beneath the black oil slick of his hairline.

Roberto Nunez's voice became cool. He was no longer amused. "If there is a mare missing from your herd then it is none of our affair."

"Your land borders mine," Vega replied. "It had to be you. I have just brought my herd in for the evening and Laeticia is gone. She was one of my favourites. A great breeding mare and I know that you have long admired her too, so do not play games with me!"

"Miguel," Roberto said stiffly. "I think you need to leave now. To accuse a man of theft in this way is a very serious business."

"But you accused me of it once!" Vega shot back.

"Yes," Roberto conceded, "but then you had stolen Nightstorm, hadn't you?"

Vega shrugged. He couldn't argue with this logic since he had indeed stolen Issie's colt.

"You have my word as a gentleman that I had nothing to do with your mare's disappearance." Roberto continued, "Our own mares were disturbed recently. Perhaps this is not an isolated occurrence. If so, then all of our horses may be in danger. Instead of charging about like madmen we should be working together to solve this problem."

Vega's lip curled beneath his moustache. The whole time he had been speaking, he had also been making furtive, greedy glances at Francoise, who sat silently at the table. "Perhaps you are right, Roberto," he said with a greasy grin, "we should work together. Perhaps the lovely Francoise might accompany me on a ride around the farm in the moonlight to look for my mare?"

Francoise had long ago learned to ignore Vega's

romantic attentions, but that never seemed to stop him from pestering her with leering stares or asking her out. She gave Vega a cool stare. "I don't think that would be a good idea. There is no point in looking for the mare in the darkness."

"What a pity!" Vega said, his eyes still fixed on her. "A moonlight ride is so romantic and you do look so lovely tonight, my dear Francoise. Your hair looks very nice."

Vega gave a bow to Francoise and then a nod to Roberto as he took his leave, slamming the door shut behind him.

There was silence at the dinner table as all eyes turned to Francoise. "That is it!" she snapped. "There will be no more talk about my hair ever again!"

Issie bit her lip but it was no good. She took one look at Alfie and the pair of them collapsed into fits of giggles.

After dinner Issie went to bed, still puzzling over the mystery of the missing horse. Normally she might have considered Vega's story to be some kind of cunning ruse to divert suspicion. And yet she didn't think so this time. She had seen the genuine fury on Vega's face when he stormed through that door, and the look of concern too. Vega was jealously possessive of his horses. He was clearly worried about the missing mare, Laeticia.

Issie lay awake for a long time thinking about this, before she eventually fell asleep. In her dreams Spanish castanets were clack-clacking away. The clacking became louder and louder and then an even louder noise jolted her out of her slumber. It was the sound of a horse whinnying. Drowsy and jetlagged, she realised that the first sound she'd heard hadn't been castanets at all, but hoofbeats on the cobblestones directly outside her balcony window.

Issie got out of bed and padded across the wooden floor to the balcony. Down below in the courtyard, illuminated in the moonlight of this warm summer night, was a grey horse. Not an enormous elegant breed like the Lipizzaners in the stallions' stables, but a pony. Not much more than fourteen hands high, and very old, with a sway back and just the slightest smattering of faded dapples on his rump. He had a snowy white face and his eyes were deep black. The pony stared up at Issie expectantly, stamping and pacing. How long had he been there? She had been in such a deep sleep and now to wake and find him here once more! She felt her heart racing.

"Mystic!" she whispered down to him. "It's OK, I'm coming!"

It took her ages to find her jodhpurs in her suitcase. As she hopped about on one foot trying to yank them on without making too much noise, Issie tried to stay calm. She needed to hurry. Mystic's arrival must mean that something was wrong. The last time he had turned up here it was to help her save Nightstorm's life. Did this mean that her stallion was in danger again?

Issie no longer questioned Mystic's instinctive ability to be in the right place when trouble was brewing. The grey pony acted as a guardian both to Issie and her horses. It had been that way ever since the fateful day, almost four years ago at Chevalier Point Pony Club. Issie and Mystic had been trying to herd a group of runaway ponies back from the main road when the accident happened. Issie had risked her life to save the ponies and if it hadn't been for Mystic rearing up to protect her, throwing her clear of the path of the truck, she would have undoubtedly been killed. Issie had been devastated when she woke up in a hospital ward to discover that Mystic had taken the blow of the oncoming truck in her place and paid the ultimate price for his bravery.

Losing her beloved pony had left Issie's heart shattered in a million pieces. She truly believed she would never recover. But then she was forced to pull herself together when Avery turned up with Blaze. The beautiful Anglo-Arab mare had been dreadfully mistreated and it was Avery's job working for Horse Welfare to find the mare a good home. Issie's heart opened up to this mare immediately. Together the girl and the horse healed each other and Issie began to ride again.

Blaze had her own secrets too. The mare had once belonged to the El Caballo Danza Magnifico and as Issie found out the truth about her, she realised just how lucky she was to have a horse as special as Blaze. As for Mystic, Issie had thought that she had lost him forever. But the unique bond that she shared with the grey pony was not so easy to break. Their destinies remained tied together and Mystic came back to her, returning whenever Issie and her horses really needed him. Not as a ghost either, but a real horse, flesh and blood, just as he was right now outside the bedroom window.

"I'm coming," Issie muttered to herself as she searched her suitcase for riding boots. In the end she gave up – it would be quieter to leave the hacienda barefoot anyway. She padded down the stairs and slipped out of the front door.

"Mystic!" she hissed. There was a nicker in reply. Mystic was standing in the shadow of the archway. She could see his coal-black eyes shining in the moonlight.

Issie ran down the steps to greet her pony, flinging her arms around his neck and breathing in his sweet, warm smell. She felt the coarse, ropey fibres of his long, silvery mane pressing into her cheek as she hugged him.

Mystic was agitated, pacing back and forth, anxious to get moving. Issie sensed the tension in him and didn't waste any more time. Using the front steps of the hacienda as a mounting block, she vaulted up on to the grey pony's back. She was accustomed to riding Mystic bareback and didn't need a bridle. Mystic would know where to go, all Issie needed to do was wrap her hands in the pony's long mane and hang on.

As Mystic trotted across the cobbles, Issie thought he was taking her to the stable blocks within the hacienda compound. The stallions, including Nightstorm, were locked away in their loose boxes, and Issie was certain that Mystic was here to protect Storm from danger – perhaps the same threat that Roberto and the others had seen off just a few nights ago.

But Mystic didn't go towards either of the stables. Instead, he trotted past the fountain, heading towards the main gate of the compound.

Issie didn't understand. If all the El Caballo horses were safe inside these walls, why was Mystic insisting on going outside?

They were right in front of the wrought iron gates when Issie heard hoofbeats approaching across the fields just outside the walls. Was it Vega with a couple of his *vaqueros*? She had encountered his cowboys before, and it was not an experience she wished to repeat out here alone in the dark.

"Come on," she urged Mystic to turn around. She didn't want a confrontation at the gates. If Vega's men were coming this way then she did not want to be waiting for them.

Mystic however, had no such fear. He stood stock still in front of the gates and raised his head high in the air, listening to the sound of hoofbeats coming closer. Issie still couldn't see anything. It was dark outside the compound and she peered into the blackness, trying to catch a glimpse of the approaching riders.

Suddenly the horses came into view. Only a few metres away, cantering straight towards the wrought iron gates!

"Ohmygod!" Issie gasped. She had feared the worst, expecting Vega's men. But the horses were not ridden by the *vaqueros*. They were not being ridden at all.

Issie had seen wild horses before, running free on the hill country of her Aunt Hester's farm. These horses approaching the gates of the hacienda were clearly untamed. Their manes were bedraggled, their coats stark from living rough and being left ungroomed. Issie could tell that the three horses were all stallions by their broad necks and powerful, muscled physiques. Each horse was quite distinct in colour and conformation.

The dun was the first one that she saw up close. He barrelled up to the gates then gave an arrogant flick of his head and veered sharply at the last minute, cantering off again. Issie took in his rugged coat, deep mustard-gold in colour with a thick, matted, chocolate-brown mane and tail. His build was stocky, with a broad neck and compact body. The black horse who followed him was larger, probably over sixteen hands high. He was not as heavy as the dun though; his physique was more refined. When he trotted right up to the gates Issie could see he had the classical, handsome profile of an Andalusian stallion.

The grey horse was the boldest of the three. He was a curious colour, a pale dove-grey with a two-toned mane that was layered black underneath and pale cream on top. He had a thick neck and noble profile and his conformation was powerful and perfect.

The dove-grey horse came up last, but came up so close that his muzzle was actually thrust through the gates. He almost touched noses with Mystic, and Issie thought at first that he was trying to be friendly. Then, without warning, the grey stallion gave a fierce squeal, and lashed out at Mystic through the bars of the gate. His ears were flat back and his teeth were bared. He began to pace up and down on the other side, desperate to get through.

Mesmerised by this stunning wild horse, Issie wanted to get closer, but she knew she needed to be careful. Gently she slid down from Mystic's back and asked the grey gelding to back up away from the gates. Then she began to approach the stallion, stepping quietly towards him. The stallion wouldn't feel so threatened if she was alone. Perhaps he might calm down.

Issie was just a few steps away from the gate, so near that she could feel the stallion's warm breath against her skin, his exhalations coming in quick, anxious snorts. She could smell the delicious sweetness of the hot horse sweat rising from his body.

"Easy boy," she said softly, extending a hand to stroke the stallion's muzzle. "I want to be friends. I won't hurt you…"

The stallion, however, was making no such promises. He raised his head in the air and let out a loud clarion call, then lunged at the gates once more, striking out between the bars and almost catching Issie with a powerful swipe of his front hoof. Issie saw the darkness in his coal-black eyes as he made a vicious lunge at her with his mouth open and teeth bared.

Suddenly the lights went on and voices were coming from the hacienda. The dove-grey horse was startled. He gave a vigorous shake of his mane and wheeled around on his hind legs. He broke into a gallop like a racehorse springing from the starting gates and disappeared into the darkness. Swept up in his wake the other two horses turned and followed. Issie listened to the hoofbeats receding as the stallions galloped off into the night.

What had she just witnessed? Wild stallions that ran as a pack? She had never heard of such a thing. A shiver ran up her spine despite the warm night air. The sound of voices filled the courtyard. But the others were too late. The stallions were already gone. And so was Mystic.

CHAPTER 5

Issie had been the only one to see the three stallions. The others rushed to join her at the gate and when Issie told them what had happened Francoise was particularly intrigued by her description of the dove-grey horse with the curious two-toned black and white mane.

"The horse you describe sounds like a Sorraia," she told Issie. "They are a wild breed here in Spain. Very beautiful and quite untamed."

"He looked like he'd never been near a human in his life," Issie said. "His mane was matted and he had rain scald and mud all over him from never being groomed."

"A wild stallion like that could be responsible for

Vega's missing mare," Avery offered, "especially if he's running with other stallions."

Roberto nodded. "After the disturbance the other night, I wonder if we are dealing with bachelors."

"Bachelors?" Issie was puzzled. "You mean like a single guy who isn't married?"

"The term bachelor does not just refer to men," Avery explained. "A horse without a mate can also be a bachelor. Bachelor stallions are young with no harem of their own. They must either challenge a stallion to take over his harem or go around in a gang stealing mares."

Issie thought about the Sorraia, with his ears flat back and his teeth bared as he tried to lunge at her through the bars of the gate. "Are they dangerous, these stallions?" she asked Avery.

"That all depends," Avery replied. "Often bachelors will assert their dominance by putting on benign displays of power – simply rearing up to look bigger than the other stallion can be enough to deter an opponent. Bachelor stallions seldom get into serious life-or-death fights in the wild. But occasionally their fights can become lethal – and when humans are involved or their herd is under threat then they will go on the attack and may kill."

Roberto smiled at Issie. "It is lucky there was a gate between you and those horses tonight," adding after a pause, "although I am surprised you made it there so quickly in the first place. I got up as soon as I heard the hoofbeats, but I did not get beyond the hacienda steps before they were gone."

"Umm," Issie faltered, "I was already awake, you know, jetlag…" She had long ago decided that she shouldn't tell anyone about Mystic, and the grey pony had disappeared into the night before anyone else had seen him.

Francoise wrapped her shawl more tightly around herself. "The horses are not coming back tonight and it is getting cold," she said. "We do not need to stand in the dark discussing this. Let's go back inside."

In the kitchen, Francoise made everyone a cup of hot chocolate before they went back to bed. It was four in the morning by then and quite a few hours of sleep had been lost. Issie took her drink and went upstairs, but now her jetlag really had kicked in. At 6 a.m. still unable to sleep, she rose again and went down to the stables.

It was only just turning light and none of the other

riders had arrived yet, so Issie had the place to herself. She walked down the corridor and opened the top door of Storm's stall. The bay stallion stuck his head out over the partition, nickering his greetings to her.

Issie's heart leapt a little. She still couldn't believe that this mighty horse was once the tiny foal that she had watched being born. This incredible stallion had been no more than a damp, bedraggled bundle, lying bewildered and newborn on the straw of Blaze's stall at Winterflood Farm. Issie had been the only one there on that stormy night when her mare had given birth, apart from Mystic. She had fallen hopelessly in love with Storm on the spot. To be reunited with him, fully grown and ready to ride at last, seemed unbelievable. If she had her way, she would be riding him right now. But she couldn't do that today. This was her first day as a pupil of the *haute école* and she needed to get ready.

She lingered a little longer at the door of Storm's loose box, taking one more look at him, absorbing every line of the stallion's magnificent body and his noble face, with the broad white blaze that made him look so much like his dam. And then, reluctantly, she shut the door and moved further down the corridor to Angel's stall.

Issie was convinced that she would be out of her depth surrounded by the El Caballo's classical riders with their incredible knowledge of the *haute école*. It made her feel a little bit better knowing that she would be riding a stallion that she truly adored and trusted with her life. After all they had a history together, her and Angel. The last time she was in Spain they had run Andalusia's deadliest street race, the Silver Bridle, and emerged triumphant.

Angel was fast, and yet he was also powerfully built, capable of performing the athletic leaps and exaggerated movements required of an *haute école* stallion. Riding an *haute école* horse was like trying to harness the power of a jet fighter with nothing more than a bridle. And yet, here in his stall, Angel was a total pussycat. When Issie entered his loose box, he came up and snuffled her sleeve affectionately.

"He's so sweet, isn't he?"

It was Francoise D'arth, leaning over the door of the stall, watching Issie and Angel. "Of course," she added, "he is not so sweet with the men. Since you were here last many of my riders have tried, but Angel still won't let a man on his back."

Issie reached up and stroked the stallion's broad snow-white neck. She understood Angel's fear and knew that the stallion would never forgive Vega for putting the *serrata* on him. In Angel's mind all men were like Vega – evil. Women were another matter. The stallion would quite happily allow Issie or Francoise to ride him.

"I have been working him regularly in the school since you left," Francoise continued. "He is one of the very best horses in the troupe, capable of the most magnificent *haute école* manoeuvres. He does the best capriole of any of them."

"I thought capriole was a pizza topping?" Issie joked.

Francoise frowned at Issie. "It is one of the 'airs above ground', Isadora – a flying leap which the horse must perform with a rider on his back, thrusting his hind legs out in a kick in mid-air."

She looked at Issie who was still smirking. "Isadora! I need to know that you will take this seriously. *Haute école* training at El Caballo is no laughing matter."

"I'm sorry, Francoise," Issie said. "I am serious, honestly. I know I need to learn this if I want to take Storm home."

Francoise sighed. "You look upon this as some kind of punishment, don't you? Perhaps, once you have learnt the true power and complexity of the art, you will change your mind."

Francoise unbolted the door of Angel's stall and stepped inside. "Come on then," she said, "Let's saddle up and take him into the arena. I'll help you to warm up and get a feel for him before the *jinetes* arrive."

The *jinetes* were the El Caballo's riders – ten of them, all selected by Francoise. "Most of them have worked in other dressage schools," she explained as they walked alongside Angel towards the arena. "Several are from my old school, the Cadre Noir in France. Others I coaxed away from the Spanish Riding School in Vienna and, of course, there are local riders from Spain too."

As they headed for the arena, Issie could see signs of life in the stables. The riders were arriving. A young boy about the same age as Alfie was mucking out one of the stalls. Francoise said a few cheery words to him in Spanish as they walked past.

"Is he one of the *jinetes*?" Issie asked.

Francoise shook her head. "The *jinetes* do not do stable chores. I have young grooms that do the mucking out. My *jinetes* do nothing but ride the stallions." She smiled at Issie. "They are the best dressage riders in the world. They have earned the right to focus on their riding."

"I don't mind yard work," Issie pointed out. "Maybe I can help to groom their horses instead of riding with them?" Issie was beginning to have cold feet about riding alongside these superhuman horsemen. Her nervousness wasn't helped by the sight of the arena itself. It had been a long time since Issie had been in this grand theatre with its perfect sand floor and tiered seating running around the walls all the way up to the enormous stained glass windows and vast, curved plaster ceiling. This was an indoor arena fit for a king – and, in fact, the King of Spain had made visits here; there was a royal box reserved just for him where he sat to watch the horses. And now Issie would be riding in with the *jinetes* in this world famous space for the very first time.

"Angel is a perfect schoolmaster," Francoise reassured her as they walked together with the stallion through the vast, wooden doors and onto the sand surface. "He is what they call a 'push-button' dressage horse. If you put your legs in the right places and give him the right commands then he will perform the most amazing tricks for you."

"Tricks?" Issie asked.

"All the *haute école* manoeuvres," Francoise said. "Do you want me to get on and show you?"

Issie gratefully handed over the reins and Francoise put her foot in the stirrup and sprang onboard. "Can you see," Francoise asked, trotting the stallion around the arena to warm up, "how his strides are naturally collected? Now watch... I will ask him to do an extended trot down the long side of the arena. I simply put my legs back a little at the girth, like this, and ask him to go!"

As she was talking, Francoise rearranged herself in the saddle and Angel suddenly picked up like a hovercraft, devouring the arena with his enormous strides. He began flicking his feet in front of him, stretching out over the ground so that he almost appeared to be suspended in mid-air. Francoise rode the extended trot down the long side of the arena and then rode up the centre line. She clucked with her tongue, moving her legs to a new position and Angel did a perfect half-pass – trotting sideways and crossing his legs over. Then she came back down the other side of the arena and did the same thing, only this time she stopped in the middle and Angel did a piaffe, trotting up and down on the spot without taking a single step forward.

Issie watched this display and felt even sicker with nerves. She had never done a piaffe in her life! Francoise made it look so easy, sitting there totally composed while Angel danced beneath her. That was the art of the *haute école* rider, Issie realised – making it all look so effortless. It was incredibly difficult to ride these manoeuvres, requiring utter precision and perfect timing.

Francoise finished the piaffe and rode Angel back over to Issie, dismounting and handing her back the reins. "There you go," she said, "you can try it." She looked up and added, "I hope you don't mind having an audience."

Issie looked in the direction of the main entrance. Standing in the doorway mounted up on their horses were four of Francoise's *jinetes*. They were watching with intrigued expressions.

"Bonjour! Jean-Jacques, Javier, Wolfgang and Franz," Francoise called out to them. "This is Isadora, the girl I was telling you about. She is joining the school for a month to train with us, and we are just having a quick preliminary lesson on Angel to get her started. If you wouldn't mind waiting there just a moment while she warms up? Then we can begin training the troupe once the others are all here." The four riders all nodded agreeably. Issie, however, felt like someone had just tied a giant knot in her belly. Not only was she going to try and perform an extended trot and a piaffe for the first time, but now she had an audience of top riders watching her do it!

"You will be fine," Francoise insisted as she legged her up. "Angel knows what he is doing. Remember to push him into your hands for the extended trot and then, for the piaffe, imagine you are holding him back, like keeping a cork in a bottle."

Issie felt herself turn rigid with nerves as she rode around the arena at a trot. She kept casting a glance over at the *jinetes*. This was an average working day for them, but for Issie it felt like the ultimate test. These world-famous riders were watching to see what she was capable of.

"Now, across the arena this time, ask him to extend the trot!" Francoise shouted out.

Issie did as Francoise told her and was amazed when Angel automatically lengthened his strides to do the same extended trot as he had done moments before with Francoise.

"Very good! Very good!" Francoise praised her. "Now down the centre line and half-pass. Left leg back behind the girth and keep the impulsion!"

Issie did exactly as Francoise instructed, clucking Angel on with her tongue to get him moving and praising him when he skipped sideways like a ballerina across the arena.

"A bit rushed," Francoise said, "keep him collected! And now bring him back for the piaffe!"

Cork in a bottle, cork in a bottle, Issie was thinking as she came down the centre of the arena. When she got to the mid-point she pulled Angel back and put her legs behind the girth as far as they would go – the signal for the piaffe. Or at least, so she thought. Angel, however, didn't read her signal that way. Rather than trot on the spot as Issie had expected, Angel rocked back on his hindquarters, snorted and rose up into the air!

Issie gave Angel a tap on his flanks with her dressage whip in the hope of getting him to drop back down on all fours. Instead, the stallion seemed to compress himself back on his hind legs, and then leapt! Issie gave a shriek as the horse bounded forward, still on his hind legs, like a bunny rabbit hopping. Later on, when she told Alfie the whole sorry story back at the hacienda, she held her hands over her face with embarrassment.

"So instead of asking him to do a piaffe," Alfie smirked, "you tapped him in the wrong spot and he did a courbette!"

Issie kept her face buried in her hands. "The worst bit is I should have just gone with it and tried to sit up and look elegant, like I knew what I was doing, like a proper dressage rider…"

"But, you didn't," Alfie grinned.

"I didn't know it was a courbette, did I?" Issie groaned. "I thought he was trying to rear up and throw me off or do something really weird. And so, after I screamed, I let go of the reins and just clung on to the saddle with both hands."

"You're kidding?" Alfie was wide-eyed with disbelief.

"I wish I was," Issie sighed. "You should have seen the *jinetes'* faces. They thought I was a loony!"

Alfie shook his head. "I wish I'd been there! Why did I skip training to go into town and get the horse feed?"

"Well," Issie said, "You'll get plenty of chances to see me making a complete fool of myself in the arena.

Francoise has scheduled me in for training every single day of the week."

"It will get better," Alfie told her kindly. "Angel is just sensitive, you'll get the hang of it. And the *jinetes* are really good guys. I have ridden with most of them for years now. They won't hold it against you. You'll see, you can learn so much from them. They're professional horsemen."

"I'm sure they are," Issie said darkly. "And I bet none of them shriek like a girl when they do the courbette."

CHAPTER 6

Issie tugged on the flouncy red flamenco skirt and pink polka-dot T-shirt and pulled a face at herself in the mirror. She never wore skirts usually and this one was laden with frills that fell all the way to the floor. She took a step and the Spanish ruffles rustled loudly as she moved.

"I look ridiculous!" she protested. "Can't I just wear my jods?"

Francoise, who was dressed in an off-the-shoulder violet dress, also floor-length with balloon sleeves, shook her head. "You know what the Spanish are like with their traditions. It is customary for us to be in flamenco dress for the *feria*."

"But how am I supposed to ride in this?" Issie groaned.

"Be thankful that you are riding!" Francoise replied. "I am being carried to the *feria* in the traditional way."

Issie wasn't sure what she meant until they got down to the stables and saw Avery waiting for Francoise, already mounted up on his horse, Sorcerer.

"Want a lift?" he asked with a grin.

Francoise reluctantly hitched up the skirts of her violet dress so that she could climb the mounting block, while Avery positioned Sorcerer alongside and held him steady so that Francoise could swing herself up on to the horse's broad rump.

"Are you comfy back there?" Avery asked.

"I would hardly say I am comfortable," Francoise complained as she arranged her skirt so that it fell in elegant tiers over one side of Sorcerer's rump, "but I am ready." She looked around with a frown. "Where are the others?"

Alfie came out of the stalls as she said this, leading a bay Lusitano.

"His name is Pepe," Alfie told Issie. "Do you remember him? We got him as a colt. He was one of the five horses that we claimed from Miguel Vega when you won the race for the Silver Bridle."

Like Storm, Pepe had grown up into a stallion. He

looked handsome with the traditional bobbles of gold, red and violet, the colours of El Caballo hacienda, that Alfie had braided into his mane.

All the horses were decorated with bobbles and braids today. Issie had been busy that morning working Storm's mane into a long running plait down his neck. She had secured colourful red, white and pink cotton bobbles along the plait to match her flamenco outfit. The stallion's bridle also had red and pink bobbles attached to it and his saddle blanket was gold, with the El Caballo insignia printed on it – the letter C with a blood-red heart inscribed in the middle.

"Come on, boy." Issie felt the butterflies in her tummy as she led Storm out of his stall and over towards the mounting block.

Storm stood patiently as she grappled with her flamenco skirt, pushing it out of the way to stick her foot in the stirrup and swing herself up into the saddle.

The thrill of being on the stallion's back was unbelievable. Finally, she was sitting astride this magnificent horse that she had raised from a baby foal.

Avery saw the look of wonder on Issie's face and smiled. "Your first ride together. It's a big moment."

"Uh-huh," Issie nodded. "I've waited so long to ride him, now it all seems so unreal—"

She stopped talking suddenly, as an even more unreal sight came round the corner of the stables.

A tubby chestnut pony with a dozy expression had plodded into view. On his back, dressed in a sunny yellow flamenco frock, with her hair worn up in a classic Spanish twist, was Mrs Brown. She was clinging to the reins, fists clenched and knuckles white. A look of total terror was plastered to her face.

Issie couldn't believe it. Her mother, who usually shrieked if a horse even came near her, was actually riding!

"Ohhh! Ohhh nooo!" Mrs Brown was trying to steer the chestnut pony towards the rest of the group, but her reins were far too long. Instead of walking in the direction that she intended, the pony had spied a stack of hay bales over by the wall and was heading straight for them.

"Ohhh!" Mrs Brown squeaked. "Stop that, Ferdinand!"

It was too late. The pony stuck his head down and began to munch on the hay.

"Pull his head up, Mum," Issie cried. "Don't let him do that!"

"I'm trying, Isadora," Mrs Brown said as she gave a futile tug on the pony's reins. "He doesn't seem to listen to me!" Mrs Brown was yanking with all her strength but Ferdinand was merrily ignoring her and tucking into the hay.

Roberto came alongside Mrs Brown on Marius and took charge of the situation. "Do not pull both reins at once," he advised her gently, "Pull on just one rein. That's right! Well done! Now keep your reins shorter, and give him a nudge with your legs."

Mrs Brown let the reins immediately slip back through her fingers and Ferdinand promptly spun around and began to eat hay again.

Roberto Nunez leapt down out of the saddle and grabbed a lead rope from the tack room. "I think perhaps to begin with we should put you on the lead rein," he told Mrs Brown as he clipped the shank of the rope on to her horse's bridle. "I'll lead you. We can ride side by side until Ferdinand learns to behave himself."

Normally when Issie and the others rode to the village, they would trot or canter most of the way, but with her mother on a total plodder, the ride to the *feria* was painfully slow. At one point Roberto suggested that they try to trot, but Mrs Brown completely failed to master the art of rising to the beat and began bouncing up and down, her hands jagging poor Ferdinand in the mouth. When Mrs Brown gave a shriek and almost slid off entirely, the trot was quickly abandoned.

"It is a lovely day for a walk anyway," Roberto said kindly, holding Marius back so that the grey horse would fall into stride beside little, tubby Ferdinand.

Issie was dying to put Storm though his paces. She had never ridden the stallion before and was desperate to know what his trot and canter really felt like.

"I can't believe it!" she muttered to Alfie. "I finally get on Storm for the very first time and I have to stick to a walk!"

"I don't think I've ever ridden this slowly in my life!" Alfie groaned in agreement. "At this rate it will take half an hour to reach the village!"

"Don't worry, Storm." Issie gave the stallion a

reassuring pat, "it won't always be this dull, I promise you." In her mind, she had pictured her first ride on her horse as a wild gallop across the countryside, not this painfully slow procession to the village. It was an anti-climax to say the least!

Mrs Brown, on the other hand, seemed to be thoroughly enjoying her first ever horseback ride. When Issie turned Storm around at one point and went back to check on how her mum was doing, she found her looking rather smug.

"This riding business is actually quite easy," Mrs Brown said. "I don't know what all the fuss is about!"

"Mum," Issie couldn't help herself, "you've got a lead rope on. You're only walking. It's hardly the Grand National!"

Although Issie and Alfie were frustrated by the pace, eventually they gave up on grumbling and began to discuss Storm and Issie's *haute école* training.

"So, how have you enjoyed your first week training with the El Caballo?" Alfie asked.

"I don't think 'enjoy' is the word exactly," Issie groaned. Since her dramatic introduction to the Spanish school when she had accidentally done a bounding courbette across the arena in front of the *jinetes*, Issie had been trying to keep a low profile at training sessions. The other riders were kind enough to treat her as if she wasn't there, which was better than laughing at her as she attempted to keep up with them.

"The *jinetes* can be hard to get to know," Alfie told her, "but they are good guys. You will see, once they accept you."

"It's not just the *jinetes*," Issie admitted. "I find the whole *haute école* thing so hard to understand. I mean, to me a trot is just a trot. But the way Francoise explains it there are all these variations – medium trot, extended trot, working trot, collected trot... I can't tell the difference! It's like she's speaking another language."

"You mean Spanish?" Alfie asked.

"No!" Issie was exasperated. "I mean when she bangs on about dressage. It's just so complicated. I feel like I'm a little kid learning to ride all over again. I'm so unco-ordinated and goofy! I try to do what she says, but I just don't think I'm ever going to grasp it."

"*Haute école* dressage takes a lifetime to master," Alfie said, trying to be kind.

"I don't have a lifetime," Issie said, "I have a month

– tops! I need to get back to Chevalier Point and start training Comet for the new season. I can't stay here forever learning twenty different kinds of trot!"

Alfie nodded. "I feel the same way when I am away on tour. It's like wherever I am in the world I feel a longing for El Caballo. Like you, I am only truly at home when I am with my horses."

Issie realised at that moment how well they understood each other, her and Alfie, even though their lives were so different. She remembered how Stella had teased her about seeing Alfie again before she left for Spain. "Stuck for a month with a cute Spanish boy?" Stella had giggled. "Poor you!"

"He's like a big brother to me," Issie insisted. "We're friends. That's all."

Issie had emailed Stella last night to check in with her best friend and ask her how Comet was coping with the rainy weather back home in Chevalier Point.

Forget Comet, Stella had moaned in reply, *he's fine! It's me you should be worried about! I'm stuck here in the rain while you're in Spain. And I know for a fact that the rain in Spain falls mainly on the plain – ha ha!*

Issie had groaned out loud at Stella's appalling joke.

Then there was Stella's reaction to the news that Issie was being forced to learn the *haute école*.

Has Francoise actually seen the way you ride dressage? Stella boggled. *Issie, you're going to be stuck there forever trying to do a fancy trot – you'll never be able to bring Storm home!*

Issie was worried that Stella was only too right.

As the white houses at the top of the hill came into view, Issie remembered the last time she had been here. The elegant town square surrounded by white houses at the top of the ridge had been the scene of her great victory in the Silver Bridle.

Today it had been decorated for the *feria*. Brilliant pots of pink and orange geraniums hung from the white buildings and colourful flags were flying from every lamp post. Around the edge of the square stalls had been erected selling hot food; the yummy Spanish egg and potato tortilla and platters of tiny, sweet, grilled pimento peppers.

This was a horse *feria* so, although a few people were

on foot, most of the villagers were on horseback. There were riders from all the local horse farms, dressed in colourful costumes. Many of the women, like Francoise, were being doubled on the back of their boyfriend or husband's horse. They chatted to their friends, passing around platters of *empañadas* pastries and *jamon* – paper-thin slices of Iberian ham – as if they were on a comfy sofa at home rather than the back end of an Andalusian stallion! Their husbands drank glasses of sherry and joked with each other as the horses beneath them stood patiently.

In the past Issie would have secretly coveted many of the magnificent horses at the *feria*, wishing they could be hers. This time, however, it was Issie's own horse that was drawing admiring stares. All the riders here today were knocked out by the stunning presence and good looks of the big bay stallion.

"You are lucky," Francoise grumbled, "I would much rather be riding my own horse than stuck here on the rump of someone else's!"

Avery grinned. "Oh come on, Francoise! Let me buy you a plate of pimentos and a glass of sherry to cheer you up."

As he turned Sorcerer to ride off towards the food stalls, he glanced back over his shoulder at his passenger. "If you want, you can put your hands around my waist."

He saw the shocked expression on Francoise's face. "I-I mean to help you keep your balance."

"There's nothing wrong with my balance," Francoise said sniffily. But she did as he suggested and wrapped one arm elegantly around his waist. Avery tapped his legs against Sorcerer's sides and they trotted off towards the pimento stall.

"Do you want me to get us some pimentos too?" Alfie asked Issie. "You can stay here if you like, I'll bring some back for you," and he trotted off after Avery and Francoise.

Mrs Brown had dismounted from Ferdinand and had tied him up to one of the hitching rails. She looked quite grateful to have her feet on the ground once more as Roberto accompanied her, strolling through the crowds towards the flamenco dancing display.

As Issie sat and waited for Alfie to return she realised she should have asked him to grab a drink as well as the pimentos. She was just about to trot over to the drinks stall when she saw a man on an enormous chestnut horse riding towards her across the square.

"Little Chica!" Miguel Vega gave her an oily grin as he cantered up to her. He was wearing the traditional *vaquero* costume and already, in the heat of the day, his shirt was soaked with sweat. Issie could see the buttons straining to contain the fat belly that threatened to escape and overlap his cummerbund.

Vega pulled out a handkerchief and dabbed at his piggy face. "So, I see our colt is all grown up? And very handsome he is too!"

Vega cheekily reached out a hand to touch Storm's bridle. The stallion, who had been so placid up until that moment, suddenly gave a high-pitched squeal and lashed out with his front leg, swiping the air and stamping his hoof emphatically back down on the ground.

"Leave him alone!" Issie said. "You know you're not allowed to come near him."

There was the clatter of hooves behind her and a moment later Alfie was at Issie's side.

"Is he bothering you?" Alfie asked, pulling Pepe up alongside Storm.

"It's OK, Alfie," Issie insisted. "I can handle this."

But Alfie wasn't convinced, and he stepped his horse forward to defend Issie from the taunts of the tubby *vaquero*.

Vega raised an eyebrow and his lips curled up in a wry grin. "It seems that the colt isn't the only one who has grown up!" he mocked. "Look at you, Alfonso! Acting like a man!"

"At least I act like a man," Alfie shot back, "not a grass snake like you, Vega."

The smile on Miguel Vega's face dropped. "Snake! You are a fine one to talk! You have stolen my best mare."

"We didn't take her!" Issie said. "It was the bachelor herd. Three wild stallions. I saw them."

Vega seemed intrigued. "Wild horses? What flight of fancy is this?"

Issie didn't get the chance to reply because at that moment Francoise and Avery came to join them. Vega took one look at Francoise in her violet flamenco dress and a lecherous grin spread across his face.

"Hey, *señorita*," he leered at her. "These children here are making up stories about wild stallions. Now why don't you tell the truth and give me back my mare?"

Francoise stiffened at his accusation. "Vega, we have already told you that we do not have her."

"All right, all right," Vega said. "Let us not argue, my sweet Francoise." He smiled at her. "You look uncomfortable up there. Perhaps you would prefer to ride with me today on the back of my horse?"

Francoise couldn't believe it.

"Come on!" Vega offered her his hand. "Ride with me! You will find my horse far more pleasant than the donkey you are on now."

Before Francoise could respond, Avery had wheeled Sorcerer around so that he was face to face with Vega.

"She's not going to be riding on your horse," he said. "She's with me. And if I were you, I would leave her alone from now on."

There was such a fierceness about Avery that Vega's smirk entirely disappeared.

"I was only joking," he said backing his horse away. "A bit of fun..." He smiled at Francoise. "I go now, but my offer remains open, *señorita*. You may ride with me on my horse anytime." And with that, he spun his chestnut stallion around and cantered off.

Avery turned to smile at Francoise, expecting her to be grateful. Instead he met with a face like thunder.

"How dare you!" Francoise fumed.

"What?" Avery was stunned, "I was standing up for you! Vega is a creep!"

"I know that," Francoise replied, "but I am quite capable of standing up for myself. I do not need a man to do it for me!"

And with that, she slid down neatly from Sorcerer's rump and began to storm off across the square.

"Francoise, wait!" Avery called after her. "This is crazy!"

"I'll tell you what's crazy!" Francoise yelled back. "Wearing this stupid dress…" She made an angry grab at the violet ruffles that were now threatening to trip her up, "… and riding on the back of your horse when I should have brought my own!"

Then she turned her back on Avery and flounced off in the direction of the gates.

"What about the pimentos?" Avery called after her.

"Eat them yourself!" Francoise snapped. "I am walking home."

Issie and Alfie watched her go in disbelief.

"Well," Alfie shook his head in amazement. "This is certainly the most exciting *feria* I have ever been to!"

He turned to Issie and handed her a platter. "Pimento?"

CHAPTER 7

Issie was fast asleep when a hand crept over the blankets and grasped her by the shoulder. She sat up with a jolt.

"Ohmygod, Alfie! You scared me half to death!"

"Sorry, but I've been trying to wake you for ages!" Alfie replied.

Issie could see that Alfie was already dressed in his jodhpurs and boots. Why was he ready so early? "We don't have to be at the riding school until ten."

"I know," Alfie said, "but I've got to take a herd of mares out to the upper fields to graze this morning and I thought you might like to saddle Storm up and come with me. We didn't really get the chance for a proper ride yesterday."

Issie was suddenly wide awake. "Give me two

minutes," she said excitedly, jumping out of bed.

Alfie smiled. "I'll meet you down at the stables."

At six in the morning the sun had risen, but there was still a chill in the air as Issie walked briskly towards the stallions' quarters. She found Alfie in one of the stalls saddling a big, black horse that Issie recognised immediately as Victorioso, the jet-black stallion that had once belonged to Miguel Vega. El Caballo had claimed this stallion as part of their prize when Issie won the Silver Bridle and it had irritated Vega greatly. The black stallion was the fastest horse in his stables. Victorioso was built for speed and every inch of his muscular physique showed that he was a true athlete.

"I thought we might want to go for a gallop," Alfie said, explaining his choice of mount. "I need a horse than can keep up with Storm."

Issie knew she should saddle Storm up quickly as Alfie was waiting. But if she had her own way, she would have spent ages just standing there and taking in the beauty of the big, bay stallion. Every time she looked at Storm she found new things that marked out the special qualities of her horse. Today, when she looked at Storm's big brown eyes, she noticed how long his eyelashes were. Then she noticed how his dark bay ears turned black at the very edges, almost like someone had drawn an ink line around them. She ran a hand down the stallion's neck and Storm turned to nuzzle her affectionately.

"Want to go for a real ride?" Issie asked her horse. She threw on the saddle blanket and lifted up the heavy Spanish saddle, then cinched the girth and lowered the stirrup irons before slipping the bridle over Storm's head, doing up the straps and leading him out into the corridor to mount up.

Storm seemed to realise that this was going to be a different kind of outing today. The stallion's blood was up and he danced and crab-stepped as Issie tried to hold him steady. In the end, she gave up trying to hold him still and simply flung herself from the mounting block so that she was lying across the saddle. Then, as the horse moved off, she swung a leg over and managed to get herself upright and her feet in the stirrups.

Alfie passed her Victorioso's reins. "Take him for me while I go and bring out the mares. I'll meet you at the gates."

Issie rode to the front gates on Storm, leading Victorioso by her side. A moment later she heard the sound of hooves chiming out against the cobblestones. Alfie was walking towards her, leading nine mares. The mares were roped together in the classic style of a Spanish cobra, with head collars linked from one to the other with ropes, in three rows of three. Alfie undid one of the ropes so that the cobra was split into two and passed the end of this rope to Issie, taking his reins back and mounting up on Victorioso.

"We'll lead them as far as the gorge," he explained. "Then we'll let them loose and drive them the rest of the way between us."

Outside the gates, on the dusty path that wound around the white stone walls of the compound, the mares settled in alongside the two stallions, and Alfie and Issie began to trot. This was the first time that Issie had ever trotted Storm and she was amazed to feel the length and elevation of his stride. Storm had paces that were as light as air and graceful as a ballerina.

"He has the same movement as Marius – big, floating strides," Alfie noted admiringly as he rode alongside on Victorioso.

Issie was also surprised at how easy it was to control four horses like this, as well as the one she was riding.

The El Caballo mares were accustomed to being driven in a cobra. They trotted together, keeping pace with Storm, as they left the dusty track and headed out over the green pastures of the lower fields of the hacienda. Ahead of them were the open, broad pastures that led all the way to the narrow gorge that divided the upper and lower grazing lands.

"Why aren't we letting them graze here?" Issie asked as they rode on. "The grass looks good."

Alfie shook his head. "We reserve these pastures for mares who have just had their foals. These mares have not foaled this season so they get the second-best grazing, on the upper pasture."

They kept the mares moving, past the wild olive trees, their boughs sagging with ripe fruit, until they reached the foothills and had to slow down as the terrain became rocky underfoot. Ahead of them was the narrow gorge that led through from the lower grazing of El Caballo to the upper pastures. The rocky pathway cut its way between bare sunburnt cliff faces, with an entrance marked by grey boulders on either side.

Alfie slid off Victorioso's back and undid the ropes on the cobra so that the mares were no longer linked to one another.

"We can drive them through from here in single file," Alfie explained. "The gorge is not wide enough to travel as a cobra. You take the lead and the mares will follow you. I will bring up the rear."

Issie rode into the gorge and Margarita went behind her with the other mares all following her lead and Alfie at the back making sure the mares did not change their minds and turn around. Not that turning around was easy within the narrow confines of the gorge. The path was not much wider than two horses and a sheer rock face rose high on either side of the path.

The horses were working up a sweat and Issie could see white foam on the reins where they had rubbed against Storm's neck. The stallion loved being at the front and he held his head high, his muscles quivering with the excitement of going somewhere new, as they rounded the bend of the gorge and the track began to widen again. The open plains spread out ahead of them.

"We are almost through," Issie called back to Alfie. "What happens when we reach the pasture?"

"You can let the mares go," Alfie replied. "They will

graze here for the rest of the day and we will return at night to bring them home."

Issie pulled Storm to one side and let the mares trot past her out on to the flat plains of the upper pastures. Here El Caballo's own grazing lands abutted Vega's vast estate. The grassy land was good for horses, so it was no great surprise that two of the most powerful and influential horse farms in Spain should be right next to each other like this, side by side.

In the distance, Issie could make out the roofline of Vega's hacienda, its turrets poking up above the orange grove and the stone walls of the estate.

Alfie had pulled Victorioso up alongside Storm and was busily unstrapping a cowhide-covered canteen from the front of his saddle. He unscrewed the lid and took a deep gulp of water, then passed it to Issie.

But Issie didn't take it from him. She was distracted, staring out across the pasture, as if she were looking for something.

"I can hear horses," she said.

Alfie frowned. "Well that's hardly surprising is it? We are riding horses, and we've got nine mares with us!"

"No!" Issie hissed, "Listen! I mean I can hear horses

coming towards us. They're moving fast."

As she said this, the sound of hoofbeats became quite clear on the morning air. There were horses coming in their direction, currently hidden out of sight behind the hills.

The hoofbeats grew louder, and then, over the brow of the hill, the most stunning sight came into view. Three horses galloping wild, their heads held high and their manes flying in the wind.

"The stallions!" Issie gasped as she recognised them. "Those are the horses that I saw outside the El Caballo gates that night!"

At the front of the herd ran the grey stallion with the two-tone mane. In the daylight the strange dove-soft colour of his coat was even more remarkable.

"Francoise was right! It's a Sorraia!" said Alfie, transfixed by the beauty of the grey horse.

Beside the Sorraia, galloping and matching him stride for stride, was the dun stallion. Now that Issie could get a good look at him she recognised he was a typical Lusitano, similar in conformation to Alfie's horse Pepe, with a Roman nose, a wide chest and short legs. At the rear was the biggest of the three stallions. He was jet black, just like Victorioso, and also solidly built, with the arched neck and haughty presence of a classical Andalusian.

Issie was puzzled. "What about Laeticia?" she asked Alfie. "I thought they had taken Vega's mare? She should be with them."

Alfie urgently gathered his reins. "They must have a hiding place where they are grazing. They would not bring mares with them like this. They are on a mission. This is a raiding party."

Issie suddenly realised what Alfie meant. The stallions were heading for the El Caballo mares that they had just let loose. They were planning to steal more mares to build up their own harem!

"Alfie," Issie was horrified, "we have to get the mares back before they—"

Her words were drowned out by a piercing stallion's cry. Not from the three stallions who were approaching, but from the horse beneath her. Storm had his head raised, erect and bristling at the sight of the oncoming marauders. He stamped and pawed at the ground and let out another battle cry, challenging the three stallions to take him on.

"Storm! No!" Issie kicked him firmly and tugged at

the reins, but Storm was completely oblivious to her efforts. Nothing Issie could do would distract him.

He gave a third whinny in the same challenging tone and this time the black stallion returned his call. Responding to the young bay stallion's taunts, he began cantering in Issie's direction.

Meanwhile, the other two wild stallions were occupied with the mares. Issie shifted her glance from the black stallion for a moment and caught sight of the Sorraia circling the herd, his ears flat back as he lunged at Margarita, nipping at her flanks, trying to separate her from the other mares.

Margarita gave a squeal and shook her head disdainfully, baring her teeth at him. The dun stallion, however, had come to the support of the Sorraia and was now flanking her on the other side, rearing up and swiping viciously with his front hooves. The rest of the herd abandoned Margarita and scattered in every direction, leaving the poor mare to fight alone.

Issie meanwhile was still struggling, as Storm continued to ignore her efforts to make him move.

"Get him out of there!" Alfie shouted. He had been racing to the aid of the mares, but now he was cantering back to help her. "The black stallion is going to attack!"

"I'm urghhh… I'm trying!" Issie grunted as she tugged again on the reins. The bay stallion's eyes were on fire. His blood was up and he wanted to fight.

"STORM!" Issie was getting hysterical and was almost in tears. The black stallion had abandoned Margarita to the others and his eyes were fixed on Storm. He pulled to a sudden halt and propped back on his hindquarters just a few metres away from Issie and her horse, assessing this young stallion, considering the best way to launch his attack.

"Issie!" Alfie's pleas were getting more desperate, "We've got to go!"

"I can't!" Issie shouted back. "He won't move!"

She was struggling desperately, but Storm was consumed by his anger and totally ignoring her tugs on the reins and impassioned attempts to turn him around.

There was a squeal from the black stallion and he rose up on his hind legs. As Storm rose up to face him, Issie shrieked and clung to his mane.

Alfie shouted, "Now! You have to act now! Turn him while he's on his hind legs! Do it!"

Issie pulled herself together, gritted her teeth and seized

her chance. Catching Storm off-balance in mid-air, she yanked hard on the left rein and spun him around. In one fluid movement, she lifted her own legs as far away from the stallion's sides as she could and brought them in with a wallop, kicking hard on Storm's flanks so that he leapt forward in shock.

The jolt was enough to bring Storm back to his senses. He began listening to his rider once more and Issie was able to ride him back towards the gorge, urging him into a gallop, away from the black stallion.

"Wait!" Alfie called after her, "We need to get the mares!"

The Sorraia and the dun had taken Margarita, but the others could still be saved. Issie galloped a wide loop, circling and driving the mares back towards the gorge. As she was doing this, she thought for a moment that she could hear the black stallion's hoofbeats behind her. She was terrified that Storm would lose his cool for a second time and she'd be embroiled in a fight once more.

"You go ahead!" Alfie yelled at Issie. "The mares will follow you – I'll drive them from the back!"

Issie didn't need to be told twice. She aimed Storm at the entrance to the gorge and galloped him hard. As they entered the narrow gorge she felt a rising wave of panic. What if the black stallion attacked from behind? She would have no way to escape; nowhere to run. She was relieved when she checked over her shoulder and saw that only the mares were following her. Alfie was right behind them too and the black stallion was nowhere to be seen. He must have given up the fight and turned to follow his bachelor gang in the opposite direction instead.

Issie was shaking with fear and didn't dare slow down out of a canter, even through the twistiest bits of the gorge. By the time she emerged out the other side, she was shaking with exhaustion and Storm was quivering and wet with sweat.

"Are you OK?" Alfie asked. He looked as traumatised as she felt.

"They came out of nowhere," Issie began, "and Storm wouldn't listen. He just wanted to fight and…"

"It's OK," Alfie told her. "They're gone now."

But it wasn't OK, and they both knew it. The stallions had gone all right – but they had taken Margarita, the favourite mare of El Caballo Danza Magnifico, with them.

CHAPTER 8

The sound of horses' hooves clattering across the cobbles in the courtyard brought Roberto and Avery running.

"What happened?" Roberto asked as Issie and Alfie pulled their horses up in front of the hacienda. "You were supposed to take these mares to the upper pastures."

"We did," Alfie said, vaulting down off Victorioso, "but we ran into trouble."

"Vega's men?" Roberto asked.

"No," Alfie shook his head. "Not men. Horses. The three bachelor stallions. They came out of nowhere in broad daylight and raided the mares…" Alfie paused, terrified to say the next words, "… they took Margarita."

Roberto Nunez's expression turned stony.

"Dad, we tried to get her back," Alfie stammered, "but there were three of them. Storm tried to fight and Issie was barely able to hold him. I had the rest of the mares to think about…"

"… and so you ran?" Roberto looked sternly at his son. Then he reached out and put a hand on his shoulder. "Well done. You did the right thing. One bachelor stallion is a treacherous proposition. To take on three of them in a fight would have been madness. You might have lost all our mares, or worse, you might have lost a life."

"A wild stallion should never be confronted," Avery agreed. "You did the right thing getting out of there." He turned to Issie. "You're not hurt?"

Issie shook her head. "I'm fine, Tom," she said. "It was a bit scary for a moment there. Storm tried to fight the black stallion, I couldn't control him."

"That was quite a technique you used to get away!" Alfie told her.

"You mean the monster kick I gave him?" Issie looked embarrassed. "Tom, I'm sorry, but I had to use the pony-club kick!"

Alfie looked blank so Avery explained, "It's a vicious wallop with your boots into your pony's side that I refer to as 'the evil pony-club kick'."

"And it's totally outlawed to kick your pony like that at Chevalier Point Pony Club," Issie continued.

"I'll let you off this time," Avery said, "since it seems to have saved your life."

"I suppose you don't have a lot of wild stallions to escape from at pony club," Alfie said.

"No, but occasionally we need to get away from Natasha Tucker!" Issie grinned.

"What is a Natasha Tucker?" Alfie asked.

"Come on," Issie said, "I'll tell you all about her while we untack the horses."

Mrs Brown had been shocked when she heard about Issie's close call with the stallions. Francoise was too; but not so shocked, Issie noted, that she was willing to let them off training. "You're due in the arena at eleven," she reminded Issie and Alfie. "Be there with your horses tacked up, ready to begin."

The El Caballo's warm-up sessions had been a bit of an eye-opener for Issie. In the stables as they were mounting up the *jinetes* would chat and laugh together, but once they were in the arena the men were deadly serious and focused. They all spoke English when they were schooling but even so, the horse terms that they used made it impossible for Issie to understand what they were saying.

"He's a bit croup high, pick him up!" one of the *jinetes* said as he watched a young horse being worked. "Now he is on the forehand," another said, "sit him back with a half-halt!"

The talk would go on like this throughout the sessions. If a *jinete* offered Issie advice, she would nod and try to do what they said, but mostly she was baffled by their instructions. Today, after half an hour of training, she gave up entirely and halted Angel in the centre of the arena, totally confused.

"Is there a problem?" Francoise asked.

"I need a translator!" Issie groaned. "I don't understand what the *jinetes* are talking about half the time, so how can I possibly ride with them?"

"Riding isn't about knowing the words," Francoise frowned, "it's about developing your feel."

"But how can I when I don't know what I'm supposed

to be feeling?" Issie was trying not to get upset, but she hated being constantly out of her depth.

Francoise, who had been standing in the arena holding Marius by the reins as she directed the other riders, now mounted up on the big grey so that she was sitting alongside Issie.

"Alfie?" she called out across the arena. "Can you run the school for the rest of the session? Issie and I are going for a ride."

Outside the El Caballo walls the mares and their foals were grazing happily on the lower pastures. Issie noted that two *vaqueros* had been assigned to stand watch over them, just in case the bachelor stallions struck again.

"Roberto is taking no more chances," Francoise confirmed, as they exited the gates and rode around the dusty trail beside the white walls of the estate.

"Any news about Margarita?" Issie asked.

Francoise shook her head. "Roberto sent men out this morning, but they haven't come back yet. I do not hold out much hope. There are too many places in the hills for horses to hide away. These stallions have survived in the wild for a long time. They will not be easy to hunt down."

She smiled at Issie, "Anyway, I didn't bring you out here to hack and chat in the sunshine. We are here to do dressage."

Issie was puzzled. "Why didn't we just stay in the arena?"

"Your mind was feeling trapped by the boundaries of the school," Francoise explained. "You think dressage is something that can only be performed by *jinetes* on a perfect sand surface. But dressage is crucial to good riders at all times. Try not to think about it," Francoise said. "Just follow me and do as I do."

The two of them were riding now beyond the grazing land towards a grove of olive trees in the distance.

As they trotted along the sandy path that led towards the trees, Francoise asked Marius to go into a collected trot. "Collect Angel up, please, a nice medium trot," Francoise said. She looked over at Issie. "Now you need to do a half-halt."

This was one of the terms that had puzzled Issie earlier.

"I am not surprised," Francoise smiled, when Issie told her this. "Even the best riders have trouble defining the half-halt. Think of it as telling the horse to wait and prepare for the next instruction."

As they kept trotting, Francoise explained more terms to Issie, and as she explained, she asked Issie to perform each of them on Angel.

Often she rode in front of Issie and showed her how a movement should look before Issie had a go herself. "This is a leg yield," she said, making Marius trot sideways, crossing his legs as he zig-zagged down the sandy path.

"Put your leg back behind the girth and ask Angel to leg yield until you reach me," Francoise called back over her shoulder. "When you are at the end of the path, ask him to canter."

Issie did as she was told.

"Now to practise our flying changes! Follow me!" Francoise called back. She was cantering Marius across the fields towards a grove of olive trees planted in neat rows. Once she reached the first tree, Francoise began to weave her way through them. Each time Francoise passed an olive tree she asked Marius to perform a flying change, so that the horse was swapping legs in mid-air as he cantered through the grove.

Issie cantered after Francoise and wove her way

between the olive boughs, Angel doing flying changes at every turn. She found herself performing the leg changes with an ease that she would never have considered possible in the arena, where she was constantly aware of the scrutinising eyes of the *jinetes*.

For the past week she had felt self-conscious, clumsy and useless, but here, with Angel responding so beautifully to her and the sun shining down as they rode, Issie felt the thrill of riding a brilliantly schooled horse and getting the best out of him.

Angel was snorting with exhilaration and Issie's eyes were shining as they pulled to a halt alongside Francoise and Marius at the far end of the olive grove.

"That felt amazing!" Issie beamed.

Francoise nodded, "And now we will go back again through the trees," she said, "but this time I want you to do half-passes to weave between them."

"OK," Issie replied, and then asked, "umm, Francoise?"

"Yes, Issie?"

"What's a half-pass?"

After they had mastered the half-passes through the trees, they rode back around the far side of El Caballo's great white walls, doing shoulder-ins and flying changes the whole way home. By the time they had reached the wrought iron gates of the hacienda Issie was exhausted.

"That was the best dressage lesson I have ever had!" she told Francoise gratefully as they dismounted and led the horses back towards the stallions' quarters.

Francoise nodded. "You ride dressage far better than you think. Very soon you will be ready to progress to the next level."

Issie wondered what she meant by this and Francoise explained. "What we did today was standard dressage. But the real art of *haute école* is far more advanced." She stared straight at Issie. "To be an El Caballo dressage rider you must be ready for war."

In the dining room that evening, Avery explained what Francoise's comment meant.

"*Haute école* horses are trained for war," Avery told Issie as they sat together waiting for the others to arrive for dinner. "Hundreds of years ago, when the *haute école* was first invented, its only purpose was warfare. Horses were trained to perform the 'high school' movements in preparation for battle."

Issie screwed up her face. "I don't get it. How is *haute école* useful in a fight?"

"The mounted soldiers would use the manoeuvres to attack their enemies," Avery explained. "They would ride a levade, where the horse rears up on his hind legs, allowing his rider to thrust a spear into a man below him. Or they would ride the capriole, making the horse leap into the air over the front lines of the opposing army and lash out with his hind legs to strike any opponents trying to approach from the rear. These were lethal manoeuvres. The original *haute école* horses were highly prized as battle machines."

"Poor horses!" Issie was horrified. "It must have been awful going to war. Horses don't want to fight anyone."

"Apart from those stallions that tried to fight you this

morning," Alfie pointed out to her as he joined them at the table.

"Well that's not the same thing, is it?" Issie said. "They just wanted to steal our mares and have a harem of their own."

"And Vega's mares too," Alfie added.

The conversation was interrupted as the dining-room door opened and Francoise walked in. "Bonsoir!" she said brightly to the rest of the dinner guests.

"Wow, Francoise," Issie said, "you look amazing."

Francoise was not normally the sort to dress up. Her dinner outfit usually consisted of jodhpurs and a cotton shirt. Tonight, however, she wore an elegant cocktail dress in soft, pale yellow silk. The dress was belted with a vintage jewelled tie at the waist. In her hair, Francoise wore a tortoiseshell comb intricately hand-carved into the shape of a flower.

"Thank you, Issie," Francoise said.

"Yeah, you look gorgeous!" Alfie agreed.

Francoise nodded her thanks and cast a furtive glance at Avery, who was sitting opposite her, but he didn't say anything. In fact he barely acknowledged her presence and stood up in a hurry, heading into the kitchen mumbling something about helping to bring the food through.

"What's up with him?" Alfie muttered to Issie.

"I dunno," Issie shrugged. "He's been acting odd ever since we got here."

Mrs Brown came in carrying a big dish of seafood from the kitchen. She and Roberto had been cooking together again that evening.

"Rob has been giving me Spanish cooking lessons, so I apologise in advance if the paella isn't up to the usual standard," Mrs Brown said as she put down the huge hot platter in front of them.

"Rob?" Issie giggled, whispering to Alfie, "I've never heard anyone call your dad 'Rob' before!"

"And I've never known my dad to let anyone use his paella pan and burn it like that without hitting the roof before!" Alfie muttered back.

While Roberto made sure that everyone had enough food and drink, Avery came back in and sat down again and dinner commenced.

"Isadora, how is the training going?" Roberto asked.

"She is making excellent progress," Francoise

answered on Issie's behalf. "In another week if she works hard she will be ready to begin the *haute école*."

Roberto smiled. "I must say Francoise, you look very nice this evening. I've never seen you wear a dress to dinner before."

"It is a gorgeous gown," Mrs Brown added admiringly. "It looks amazing on you."

Francoise looked uneasy with all the compliments. "OK, so I put on a dress for once. There is no need to make a fuss!" she said dismissively. She glared across the table at the one person who wasn't making a fuss at all. Avery kept his head down over his paella.

"Well I need a new dress," Mrs Brown said, trying to lighten the mood which was now distinctly tense. "I understand there is a big dance soon?"

"The wine harvest fiesta," Roberto nodded. "It marks the end of the sherry season and it is a chance for all the village to get together."

"I'd love to go to something like that!" Mrs Brown was excited.

"And I would be only too happy to take you!" Roberto told her, adding, "It is a traditional Spanish dance, you see, so you must have a man to escort you."

"That's a bit old-fashioned and sexist isn't it?" Issie pulled a face.

Alfie shrugged. "Traditions mean everything here, Issie. You know that."

Issie was only too aware of the importance of tradition. She had been the first girl to ever ride in the Silver Bridle. Still, she respected the ways of the people here in rural Andalusia.

"You can be my date," Alfie offered. "It'll be fun. I promise."

"OK," Issie agreed.

There was silence at the table now as everyone turned expectantly to look at Avery who was strangely preoccupied with staring at his paella. Finally, he looked up at Francoise sitting opposite him in her yellow silk gown.

"The fiesta sounds like a waste of time," he said abruptly. "We are here so that Issie can learn to train at *haute école* level and take Nightstorm home. If everyone starts getting caught up in dances and harvest fiestas and heaven knows what then we'll never achieve what we came here for."

Francoise's face dropped. "It is one night!" She shook her head in disbelief. "Can you not stop thinking about horses and have fun just for one night?"

"I'm sorry but dressing up in a silly costume and flinging myself about isn't actually my idea of fun," Avery retorted.

"Ohhh!" Francoise pushed her paella plate aside and stood up from the table, utterly furious with Avery. "You, you make me so mad! You don't seem to care at all about…" Francoise suddenly realised that everyone was staring at her and finished her sentence half-heartedly, "… tradition."

Then she stormed out of the dining room.

After Francoise's departure everyone hastily finished their paella and moved to the living room to sip hot chocolate and eat *crème catalans* – thick, rich desserts that tasted of baked toffee on top and creamy custard beneath. Issie wolfed down her dessert much faster than the others so that she could wander down to the stables to say goodnight to Angel and Storm before she went to bed.

It had been a strange day, she thought, as she walked across the cobbles towards the stallions' quarters. Well, to be precise, it wasn't the day that was strange, it was Francoise. The Frenchwoman had seemed so calm and cheerful today at training, but completely lost her cool at dinner. Now that Issie thought about it, Francoise had been moody ever since they had arrived in Spain.

Issie noticed that there was a light on as she approached the stables. Perhaps one of the grooms was in there? It seemed a bit late for them to still be here. The stalls were usually in darkness at this hour.

"Hello?" Issie's voice echoed through the cavernous interior of the stallions' quarters. "Is there anyone here?"

There was silence for a moment and then a voice, at the far end of the corridor. "*Oui*, I am in with Marius."

Issie walked down to the far end of the stable block. In the last loose box, Francoise was busily grooming Marius. Still dressed in her yellow silk gown, she was furiously working a body brush over the stallion's rump.

"Francoise? Why are you out here in the middle of the night?"

"Marius needed grooming," Francoise said, bending

down to work on his legs. "And I needed to calm down and let off some steam."

Francoise stayed focused on the horse's hocks, brushing furiously.

"I told you today, didn't I, Isadora, that riding horses was all a matter of feeling?"

"Yes," Issie agreed, wondering where this was leading.

"So how can it be," Francoise asked, "that Tom Avery can be such a great rider, when that man has absolutely no feelings at all!"

"What do you mean?" Issie was totally baffled now.

Francoise began to briskly brush Marius's tail. "He is a heartless, thoughtless fool!"

Issie watched as Francoise whipped the tail back and forth, her anger building with each brush stroke. She had always known that Francoise and Tom shared a very delicate and tempestuous relationship. But things had been different on this visit. Avery and Francoise had been constantly bickering and arguing ever since they had arrived at El Caballo Danza Magnifico.

"I mean," Francoise continued her rant, "he comes all the way here and I thought he would have changed, but he is more maddening than ever! The most infuriating man!"

Francoise threw the dandy brush down on the straw of the stall floor and put her head in her hands.

Issie was shocked. She had no idea Francoise felt like this. "You really can't stand him, can you?"

Francoise turned to Issie with wide eyes. "Oh, Isadora!" she said. "It is worse than that, much worse." She paused and took a deep breath. "I think I am in love."

CHAPTER 9

"But how can you be in love with Tom?" Issie was stunned. "I mean, ever since we got here you've been totally miserable."

"I am!" Francoise agreed. "Isadora, it's all gone so wrong! I thought he loved me too but now, oh, I don't know…"

Francoise took a deep breath and then the truth came pouring out. She and Avery had started emailing each other six months ago, organising the arrangements for Storm to come home to Chevalier Point.

"It was all about the horses at first," Francoise explained, "and then we began to talk about other things. Our emails became, well, romantic…"

"Romantic!" Issie was floored. "Tom?"

Francoise nodded, "His words were so sweet. But then when he got here, it all just seemed to go wrong. I didn't know what to say, and neither did he. So we both said nothing. And now we keep getting into these stupid fights…"

Francoise sighed and dusted the horse hairs off her yellow silk dress. She picked up the dandy brush she had thrown onto the straw and put it back in the grooming kit. "He did not even notice my dress tonight," she said sadly. "And he refuses to even consider taking me to the harvest dance."

Issie was too stunned to speak. How could she have been so blind all this time? And poor Francoise! No wonder she was so upset.

"I'm sorry Francoise," Issie shook her head, "I wish there was something I could do to help."

Francoise suddenly pulled herself together and resumed her haughty composure. "There is. You can learn the *haute école* as quickly as possible and leave El Caballo Danza Magnifico and take Tom Avery away with you. Being around him is making me miserable and crazy. The sooner he is gone, the better!"

After that disastrous evening Francoise seemed to make a point of turning up at dinner in her jodhpurs and shirt, straight from the stables, as if to emphasise the fact that she could no longer be bothered. She made sure that she always sat as far away from Avery as possible and barely took part in the dinner conversations, leaving the table with haste as soon as the meal was done.

Avery, meanwhile, looked every bit as miserable and uncomfortable as Francoise. All of this was in stark contrast to Mrs Brown and Roberto Nunez who were always talking and laughing and swapping recipes for Spanish dishes. In fact Issie was beginning to wonder if her mother and Roberto were getting on a little too well. She expressed this concern to Stella in an email after dinner late one evening. Stella emailed back:

Ohmygod! What if your mum and Roberto fall in love and get married? Then you can go and live in Spain and I can come and visit you and the handsome Alfie – who will by then be your step-brother so you cannot date him of course because that would be weird, right? But I could still go out with him and he would take me in his arms and we would fall madly in love...

Typical Stella. Issie wished she'd never said anything. It was crazy to think that her mum and Roberto might be in love. Issie didn't want to move to Spain, she liked living in Chevalier Point! And the stuff about Alfie? Stella had never even met him!

What Issie regretted the most though was telling Stella about Avery and Francoise. Issie knew she mustn't mention her conversation with Francoise to anyone at El Caballo Danza Magnifico. But she figured it would be safe to blab it all to Stella in New Zealand, thousands of miles away.

Poor Francoise! Stella had written back, *I can't believe Tom has broken her heart! I am going to give him a piece of my mind when he comes back to the pony club!*

Issie was horrified. Stella was a total gossip and by the time they got home it would be the talk of the Chevalier Point Pony Club. Avery would know Issie had told them and he would want to kill her!

At least things were beginning to improve in the riding school, Issie consoled herself. Since Francoise had taken her riding through the olive grove, Issie felt like her understanding of dressage had stepped up a level. When the *jinetes* tossed out terms now, like having the horse 'between the leg and the hand', she understood what they meant. She was able to listen to their advice and join in their conversations.

Issie's favourite *jinete* was the tanned, whippet-thin, Corsican rider, Jean-Jacques. Two years ago, Francoise had found Jean-Jacques working at her old riding school, the famed Cadre Noir de Saumur, and had convinced him to come and work for El Caballo Danza Magnifico instead. Jean-Jacques didn't speak good English, but he somehow managed to convey his advice by saying very little. He was always helpful, taking Issie aside if she was having trouble mastering a manoeuvre; spending time with her and giving her tips. With his help she began to learn the piaffe and by the end of the week she had managed to get Angel to perform his first piaffe in the middle of the arena with the whole troupe watching them.

"Put the legs right back and keep the hold on reins," Jean-Jacques instructed. "Now with your heels! Sit up! And hold him! *Magnifique*, Isadora!"

The thrill of performing a perfect piaffe was unbelievable. The powerful, grey stallion stepped down the centre of the arena at a trot and then, as Issie gave him the signal, he stopped and began to trot up and down on the spot, lifting his knees high in the air but not moving forward a single inch!

"Bravo! Well done!" called out Jean-Jacques, Francoise, Alfie and the rest of the *jinetes* from the sidelines.

Francoise seemed delighted with Issie's progress. "Next week," she told her, "we will begin work on the 'airs above ground'. If you can grasp them at this rate then they should take no more than a week or two to learn. And then you may take Nightstorm home."

Two weeks ago nothing would have pleased Issie more than to have heard this news. But when Francoise said this, she felt sad somehow. Issie knew that Francoise was still upset about Avery and it seemed a shame that things had worked out this way.

After Issie's piaffe, the *jinetes* had finished training and gone home for the day and Francoise and Alfie had gone back to the hacienda. It was only 6 p.m, dinner was a long way off and the sun was still high in the sky. Issie's legs ached from a hard day's training, but even with aching legs, she couldn't resist the chance for a quick ride on Storm before nightfall.

The bay stallion nickered when he saw her walking towards his stall, craning his neck over the Dutch door and giving little whinnies of excitement.

"Did you think I'd forgotten about you, boy?" Issie said, stroking his velvet-soft muzzle over the partition door. "I'm going to take you out for a ride. I'll just get your gear out of the tack room and then we'll go."

The tack room at the El Caballo Danza Magnifico wasn't your typical pony-club affair. It was a grand, wood-panelled room at the far end of the stable block. The room was circular and at its core stood a three-metre wide, solid, wood-panelled tower that extended from the floor all the way up to the top of the high-vaulted ceiling. Carved wooden saddle racks were attached to this tower, like branches sticking out of a Christmas tree.

When Issie walked into the tack room, she didn't realise that there was someone else already in there, hidden out of view on the other side of the tower. She did, however, notice the footprints.

They weren't ordinary footprints. They were cut-outs in the shape of a man's shoe, made from brown paper and dotted about on the concrete floor at strategic intervals. The footprints were laid out in pairs, with chalk lines drawn on the concrete and arrows pointing from one pair to the next like a diagram.

Issie was baffled by the footprints. She was even more confused when she heard the tango music start up and Tom Avery's voice from behind the wooden tower, chanting over the top of the Spanish rhythms.

"Right foot forward," she heard Avery talking to himself. "One-two-three and… turn! And left-one-two-three and…"

Issie watched in amazement as Avery, completely absorbed in the patterns on the floor, tangoed his way out from behind the wooden tower. He was concentrating so hard on putting his feet in the right place and holding his hands around his imaginary dancing partner that he didn't notice Issie until he was almost on top of her.

"Isadora!" Avery practically let out a squeak and jumped backwards. "What are you doing in here?" Issie tried unsuccessfully to suppress a grin. "What are you doing?"

Avery was flustered. He bent down and began picking up the brown paper footprints that he had laid down on the floor. "I was, umm… this isn't what it looks like…"

"It looks like you were teaching yourself how to tango," Issie offered helpfully.

"Well in that case," Avery said, 'I suppose, yes, it is what it looks like."

"But I thought you told Francoise that dancing was a waste of time and you weren't interested?"

Avery looked slightly pained at being reminded of this and shook his head. "It's complicated Isadora, you wouldn't understand…"

"But I do!" Issie was excited. "You wanted to ask Francoise to be your partner but you can't actually dance! You lost your nerve and now she's not speaking to you. So you're in here, trying to learn the steps to the tango and summon up the courage to ask her to the dance."

Avery looked utterly astonished. "Umm, well, yes, I suppose that just about sums it up really…" Then he looked suspiciously at Issie. "How did you figure all this out?"

Issie smiled at him. "I can't tell you that. But if you ask Francoise to the dance, I'm pretty certain she'll say yes."

A look of cautious delight appeared on Avery's face.

"If I were you," Issie added cagily, "I would do it straight away. Ask her tonight, after dinner."

Avery looked awfully pleased. Then he realised once again how foolish he must seem with his handful of paper footprints and his iPod still playing the tango in the corner of the tack room.

"Listen, Issie, if you wouldn't mind not mentioning any of this…"

"… to Francoise? Of course I won't!" Issie said. "I won't tell anyone."

Issie made a quick dash to grab Storm's saddle, bridle and a saddle cloth off their rack and then grinned at Tom.

"Right then," Avery said. "Well? What are you still standing here for? Off you go!"

Issie could hardly contain her excitement as she tacked Storm up. Avery did like Francoise after all! It was so obvious, really. After Francoise's prickly responses to his attempts to woo her, Avery had been too shy to ask her to the harvest dance – especially since he was a terrible dancer! But now that Issie had given him the hint it seemed certain that he would pluck up the courage. She couldn't wait to tell Stella. Imagine if Francoise and Avery ended up dating! Seeing as Stella already knew, then surely there was no harm in emailing her about this new and exciting development as soon as she got back from her ride.

Issie set off around the walls of the compound, taking the same path she had taken the other day with Francoise. If she were riding Angel then she would have used this opportunity to try out her schooling tricks, doing shoulder-ins and the flying changes through the trees. But Storm was too young and green to learn such things, so she just stuck to the basics; walking, trotting and cantering, asking the stallion to listen and respond to her aids without question. She was surprised at how much better her riding had become after all those dressage lessons in the arena. Her seat was so much deeper and her balance was much better too.

She did wonder though whether she would really be able to teach Storm the *haute école* moves by herself once she got him home. It was one thing to perform them at El Caballo Danza Magnifico with Francoise or Jean-Jacques to help her, but it was quite another matter to master the moves so that you knew how to do them without an instructor at your side. Once she was home again, would she really be able to do *haute école* all on her own?

Issie still wasn't confident that she could master the *haute école* moves full stop. But she wasn't about to speak of her fears to anyone, especially not Francoise or Roberto Nunez. If they thought she couldn't handle training Storm then they would never let her take her horse back to Chevalier Point. And she wasn't going home again without her beloved stallion. Not this time.

Storm was eager for dinner by the time they got back home. He nickered and paced as he waited for Issie to mix up his hard feed. Issie loved to watch him eat, to hear his soft snuffles as he hungrily devoured his feed. By the time she had put his lightweight cotton stable rug on and left his stall, it was getting late. She hurried back to the house and found the others already gathered in the living room having tapas.

"Isadora!" Roberto greeted her brightly. "We were

just wondering where you had got to. Now that you are here we can go through to the dining room. Dinner has been served and—"

He was interrupted by a knock at the door. "Excuse me for a moment," he told the others, and he walked out into the hallway.

Issie could hear mutterings in the hall. Roberto, and another voice, a familiar one. And then Roberto called out, "Francoise, could you come here? There is someone to see you."

Francoise frowned and walked out into the hallway. Issie and Alfie, unable to control their curiosity, exchanged a glance and then slipped through to the sun lounge at the front of the house so that they could peer out through the curtains of the front window to see who it was.

"*Madre mia*!" Alfie exclaimed when he saw who was standing at the front door.

"Ohmygod!" Issie couldn't believe it either.

Standing on the doorstep, with a bunch of wilted sweet peas clutched in one chubby fist, wearing his best suit, was none other than Miguel Vega.

"What is he doing here?" Alfie asked.

They didn't have to wonder for long as they could hear every word that Vega said. "*Señorita* Francoise," Vega gave a bow, "please, these are for you." He thrust the bunch of sweet peas clumsily into Francoise's hands.

"Merci, thank you," Francoise was clearly baffled. Vega stood there staring at her.

"Is there something you want, Miguel?" Francoise frowned.

"What? Oh yes, yes, *si*!" Vega said.

"Well?" Francoise sighed. "What is it?"

"*Señorita*," Vega looked nervous. A bead of sweat ran down his brow. "It would be a great honour to me if you would accept my invitation and accompany me to the harvest dance next weekend."

Francoise looked like she didn't know what to say. She glanced back over her shoulder down the hallway, as if she was giving Tom Avery one last chance to emerge into the hall and ask her instead. But Avery did not appear. So, with a look of grim acceptance of her fate, Francoise took a deep breath and said, "All right."

Vega's eyes grew wide with shock. "All right? That means yes? *Si*?"

"Yes, *si*," Francoise said flatly.

"Excellent! Excellent!" Vega broke out in a victorious grin. "Then I shall see you here on the night. You may ride on the back of my horse with me!"

"I'd prefer to ride my own horse," Francoise clarified.

Vega nodded agreeably. "Whatever you say, my dear. It is a date!" And with that, he reached out and grabbed Francoise's hand and raised it so that he could plant an oily kiss on the top of it.

"Good night! See you then, my love!" he smiled as he backed away down the steps and mounted his horse to ride off.

As Francoise watched him go, she wiped the kiss off the back of her hand on to her jodhpurs. Her face remained stony and expressionless. Meanwhile, in the sun lounge, Issie and Alfie's faces were wide-eyed with shock and horror. Francoise D'arth had just agreed to go to the harvest dance… with Miguel Vega!

CHAPTER 10

Issie and Alfie had to make a mad dash to get back to the dining room and take their seats before Francoise came back down the hall to join them.

"What on earth are you two up to?" Mrs Brown frowned at her daughter as she sat down. "Where did you race off to?"

Issie didn't get a chance to answer. Francoise was already walking back in the door, looking rather shell-shocked.

"Well?" Roberto looked at her expectantly. "What did Vega want? He told me it was personal and he needed to speak with you alone."

Francoise sat down at her place at the table and composed herself. She looked directly at Avery as she spoke. "Miguel came here tonight to ask me to be his partner at the harvest dance."

There was a choking noise from across the table. Avery, who had been sipping on a glass of sherry, appeared to have swallowed some the wrong way and was now having a coughing fit.

"Vega asked you to the dance?" he managed to gasp out. "What did you say?"

"I told him yes," Francoise said, ignoring everyone's shocked stares and focusing on the plate of food in front of her. "This looks delicious, Roberto," she said with a stiff politeness in her voice, "I hope I did not keep you all waiting? We should eat now before it gets cold."

For the rest of the dinner Avery pushed his food around his plate distractedly, looking like he was about to explode. He had finally summoned up the nerve to ask Francoise out and Vega had beaten him to it!

Having a date for the harvest dance didn't seem to improve Francoise's mood either. She was still scowling and stroppy as she brushed down Marius before training the next morning.

"Of course I do not want to go with Vega!" Francoise snapped when Issie asked her about it. "But you know what traditions are like here. I could not go to the dance on my own. Does Tom expect me to sit there like some wallflower for the rest of my life waiting for him to notice me? No! He left me no choice but to accept Vega's invitation."

When Issie told Alfie he shook his head and groaned. "She is too proud, that is her problem. If she wanted Avery to go to the dance with her, why didn't she ask him herself?"

"It's not her fault," Issie said standing up for Francoise. "Tom had told everyone that he thought the dance was a waste of time. How could she know that he was going to ask her? He left it too late!"

After the scene at last night's dinner Issie had confided in Alfie about Francoise and Tom. She knew she really shouldn't gossip, but she trusted him. And it was nice to finally be able to share the secret.

If Stella had been here instead of Alfie, then by now they would have been working on a secret plan to bring Avery and Francoise together. But Alfie wasn't interested in being a matchmaker. "Let them sort out their own love lives," he shrugged. "We have bigger things to worry about. Like getting Margarita back."

The bachelor stallions that had raided El Caballo's herd still hadn't been found. Roberto had sent his men out in search parties, combing the terrain, but there was no sign of the stallions or the mares that they had taken.

Issie felt dreadful about losing Margarita. "If only Storm hadn't behaved like that, we might have been able to get Margarita back through the gorge to safety with the others," Issie told Alfie.

"No," Alfie shook his head, "we were outnumbered and unprepared. You do not take on a band of three bachelors. Those stallions are willing to fight – to the bitter end if necessary. We were right to run."

It was amazing how different wild stallions were to the horses here in the stables at El Caballo Danza Magnifico, Issie pondered, as she saddled up Angel for training. Angel was every bit as powerful as the wild bachelors, but his gentle temperament, training and breeding set him apart from them. After riding him in the Silver Bridle, Issie would have trusted the big, grey Andalusian with her life and over the past few weeks of intensive schooling her faith in the stallion had grown even stronger. She just hoped that she was ready to ride him to the next level.

"We will warm up today with a basic quadrille," Francoise told Issie and the *jinetes* as they lined up in the arena.

Quadrilles were a regular part of the training at El Caballo. The choreographed routines where the riders rode in perfect lines and kept time with the rider opposite them as they danced across the school were a vital part of the troupe's performance. Issie had been practising the various quadrilles with the *jinetes* for the past few weeks and she knew all of the set pieces off by heart. As Francoise gave the cue for the music to be played over the loudspeaker, Issie took her place in the line opposite Jean-Jacques and held Angel firmly, waiting to begin.

The song that came over the loudspeaker was one of the staples of the El Caballo Danza Magnifico performance, a piece of classical music called 'Zadok the Priest', full of swelling violins, just perfect for gathering the horses up and cantering half-passes across the arena. Issie did exactly that now, coming down the centre line and swishing sideways, cutting neatly in between Jean-Jacques and Wolfgang, who were cantering in the opposite direction. Then she circled around and slowed Angel to a trot in perfect step with the rest of the ride, bringing the big, grey horse back into line to cross the arena and stop in the dead centre, along with the eleven others, and perform a piaffe. Then they all changed direction and cantered the perimeter before crossing the arena on the diagonal, one after the other, doing flying changes with every second stride. Issie never missed a beat. As the music ended and the riders lined up to take their bows to an imaginary audience, Issie was shaking with exhaustion and exhilaration. It had been a perfect performance!

Francoise clearly thought so too. "Nicely done, everyone," she gave them a round of applause.

She came over to Issie and took hold of Angel's reins. "I think you are ready to try the 'airs above ground' today."

"Really?" Issie squeaked. She was pleased that Francoise thought she was ready, but still felt terrified at the prospect.

"We'll begin with the levade," Francoise said. "Watch Jean-Jacques, he will show you how it is done."

Jean-Jacques brought his horse, Trieste, over to demonstrate the manoeuvre for her. He pulled the horse to a halt in front of Issie and Francoise and then positioned himself with his legs well back. Using his dressage whip to tap the horse on the shoulder, he asked the stallion to go up on his hind legs. Trieste, an elegant grey with a very dark, steel-coloured mane and tail, neatly obliged, rocking back on his hocks and lifting his front legs up off the ground so that they were tucked up in the air, like a dog begging for treats. As the horse reared up, Jean-Jacques barely moved in the saddle. He sat calm and still as Trieste held the pose, and then, after a few moments, he tapped the stallion's front leg lightly with his dressage whip. Trieste lowered back down so that he was on all fours once more.

"Perfect!" Francoise said. "That is the levade. Isadora, why don't you try?"

Issie rode Angel into the centre of the arena and Francoise stepped forward to stand right up close to the grey stallion.

"You put your leg here," she said, gripping Issie's

calf muscle firmly and guiding her leg into position. "Your hands must be perfectly still and up high. Now you give him a nudge, but your hands hold him back. Good! Tap his shoulder with the whip to let him know you want him to go up on his hindquarters."

Issie gave Angel a tap and the stallion snorted indignantly and leapt forward! Issie managed to hang on and turned Angel around and brought him back into position to try again.

"Do not startle him with your whip," Francoise told her. "Give him regular little taps, like this." She took the whip from Issie's hands and tapped Angel with tiny flicks on his shoulder. Angel immediately understood what was being asked of him. He rose up on his hind legs and Issie felt the strangest sensation as he lifted up beneath her. She panicked for a moment that she was going to slide backwards out of the saddle and down his rump!

"You won't," Francoise reassured her when she said this. "Keep your position exactly the same. Do not move – let Angel find his balance. There you go! Perfect."

Angel was balanced on his hind legs, his front legs tucked under his chest.

"Now tap his leg to let him know you are ready to come back down," Francoise instructed, handing her back the whip.

Issie tapped his leg and Angel lowered his front legs back down on to the sand floor of the arena.

"Very well done!" Francoise enthused. "Now the courbette!"

This was the *haute école* move that Issie had performed by mistake on her first day in the school when she was asking for an extended trot.

"You must have tickled him by mistake with the dressage whip on his flank," Francoise pointed out. "That is the cue to leap up and do a courbette."

Even though she had previously managed to do it accidentally, when Issie tried to do the courbette this time it was much harder than the levade. Issie had to get Angel to rear back and then once he was balanced on his hind legs she had to tickle his flank to make him bunny hop across the arena.

There were several failed attempts as Angel went up on his hind legs, but failed to leap. Jean-Jacques tried to help, showing Issie how it was done on Trieste and eventually, with Francoise wielding the whip on her behalf, Issie managed to get one desultory hop out of Angel before he dropped back down with all four legs on the arena's sand surface once more.

"Not bad for your first time," Francoise insisted, but Issie could hear the hesitation in the trainer's voice. It had been a ham-fisted attempt and Issie knew it.

"The last one that we will try for today is the capriole," Francoise told her. "Just watch as Jean-Jacques does it. That will give you the idea and then you can try it."

Jean-Jacques took Trieste into the middle of the arena to prepare for the capriole. He balanced the stallion on his hind legs, then, unleashing the horse's power in a swift and sudden movement, he urged Trieste on to take a flying leap through the air. In mid-air the horse did a stunning ballerina kick with his hind legs, thrusting them out behind him before he gathered himself up and landed back down on the ground again.

Issie was amazed. "I don't think I'll ever be able to do that," she sighed.

Francoise was not so defeatist. "It is just hard training and focus." She wasn't about to let Issie off the hook. "Your turn. Bring Angel into the centre of the arena."

She saw the nervous look on Issie's face and tried to

reassure her. "You know how to do this. A tap on his shoulder to make him go up on his hindquarters, then one on his rump to jump up and a third tap lower down on his hind leg to make him kick out in mid-air, OK?"

As Issie rode Angel back out into the centre of the arena she tried so hard to listen to what Francoise was saying, to follow Jean-Jacques's example and think of everything she had to remember. She was shaking so much with nerves that it was hard to keep a steady hand on the reins.

"Keep calm," Francoise was saying. "Concentrate on your timing and your preparation…"

In the middle of the arena, Issie brought Angel to a halt and prepared to do the capriole. She put her legs in what she hoped was the right position and when she thought the stallion was ready she tapped his shoulder to get him up on his hindquarters and then brought the dressage whip down briskly on his bottom as Francoise had instructed. She expected Angel to leap into the capriole. But instead he simply bolted, panicking and breaking into a gallop down the length of the arena. Issie tried to hang on, but she had lost her stirrups and in the shock of the sudden gallop she lost her reins.

"Pull him up!" Francoise shouted. But it was too late. Issie slipped down the side of the saddle, made a futile attempt to regain her balance and felt the ground rushing up to meet her. The crash was even worse for its inevitability. She tried to roll with it, but still felt the hard crunch in her shoulder and the wind knocked out of her. By the time Francoise reached her side Issie was standing up and brushing herself down.

"Your timing was all wrong," was the first thing that Francoise said to her. "You need to tap him with your whip at the same moment that you give with the reins."

Yeah, I'll try and remember that next time, Issie thought sourly as she dusted the sand off her jodhpurs.

Angel had stopped galloping at the end of the arena and Jean-Jacques had caught the horse and brought him back to Issie. Despite her reservations, Issie mounted up again and prepared herself for another try.

"Keep him steady," Francoise instructed as Angel went up on his hind legs. "Now! Tap his rump with the whip and let go!"

This time, as the ground rushed up to meet Issie once more, at least she wasn't surprised.

CHAPTER 11

El Caballo Danza Magnifico's flying stallions were not the only performing horses in the troupe. The Spanish school also trained Anglo-Arab mares. Issie clearly remembered the very first time she saw these magnificent dancing Arabians perform when they came to Chevalier Point, and her amazement when she discovered that her own pony, Blaze, had once been the most beloved mare of Roberto Nunez and El Caballo Danza Magnifico. Blaze's bloodlines were shared by many of the Anglo-Arab mares here at the Spanish stables, so when Issie saw Francoise leading a liver chestnut mare down the corridor of the mares' stables, she was not surprised to see that she was a dead ringer for Blaze.

"This is one of Blaze's half-sisters," Francoise confirmed. "Her name is Amira. It is Arabic for 'princess'."

"Hello Amira," Issie smiled, reaching out a hand to stroke the mare's white blaze. "I'm a friend of your big sister."

"You will be riding Amira this evening to the harvest dance," Francoise explained. "It is traditional for women to ride on the back of their boyfriend or husband's horses. If a woman chooses to ride on her own horse, however, then custom decrees that she must ride a mare."

"Do you hear that Amira?" Issie giggled. "It's a girl's night out! No boys allowed!"

Amira snorted, as if she found it amusing too. The mare stood patiently while Issie mounted up. Francoise, meanwhile, had gone back into another stall and now she emerged again, with yet another chestnut mare that also looked like Blaze.

"Another half-sister," Francoise said. "This one is called Aliya."

She mounted up. "This dress is not very comfortable for riding in. My corset is too tight!" She fiddled with the bodice on her brilliant vermilion gown and adjusted the rose in her hair. They had all gone in to the village earlier that day to buy new flamenco dresses and Issie had picked a bright blue dress with stiff wire threaded through the ruffles of the skirt. It stuck out in enormous petals as she sat there on her horse.

"Is Mum riding one of the mares too?" Issie asked nervously. Mrs Brown might have been full of bravado about her new-found riding skills, but Issie was worried that her mother wouldn't be able to handle a highly-strung, sensitive Arabian. These were not beginners' horses and they required expert handling.

"It's OK," Francoise said, seeming to read Issie's mind, "your mother has decided to travel to the dance in the traditional way."

As Francoise said this, Roberto appeared on the grey stallion, Marius. Tucked in behind him, with her arm tight around his waist, was Mrs Brown. She looked a little nervous, riding side-saddle in her dark green, lacy flamenco dress, but Roberto was clearly quite happy with the arrangement and looked pleased to have a passenger on board.

"Your mother has become quite the horsewoman since she got here," Francoise noted.

Issie shook her head in disbelief. "All these years I've tried to get Mum keen on horses, but there was no way. And now look at her!"

"What are we talking about?" It was Alfie, who had joined them on Victorioso.

"The incredible powers of Roberto Nunez," Issie grinned. "He's managed to actually get my mother on a horse – twice now!"

"My father can be very persuasive," Alfie smiled, "and he really enjoys your mother's company."

Roberto and Mrs Brown looked over and spotted the other riders watching them. Issie's mum gave them a wave. "You look lovely, sweetie!" she called out.

"Are we ready to go then?" Roberto asked.

Alfie frowned. "So Avery's really not coming with us?"

Issie shook her head. "He says he has too much work to do, making enquiries and sorting out the paperwork for shipping Storm home."

"What about Vega?" Alfie asked.

Francoise looked less than pleased at the mention of his name. "There is no need for us to turn up together," she harrumphed. "I told him he could meet me there."

They all set off across the courtyard, the horses' hooves tap-tapping like castanets on the cobblestones. When they reached the wrought iron gates Issie saw Francoise look back longingly at the hacienda, as if she were hoping that Avery might change his mind and come after all. But the doors of the villa remained resolutely shut.

"Come on," Francoise sighed and gave up at last, turning her back on the hacienda. "Let's go to the dance."

The village square looked amazing. Streamers and fairy lights had been strung from every building and every tree. On the front of the town hall, where the dance was being held, coloured lights had been hung on either side of the ancient wooden entrance and rose petals were sprinkled over the stairs that led inside.

Since everyone was arriving on horseback this evening, there was already very little space left at the hitching posts nearest the hall. Issie and the others from El Caballo had to lead their horses all the way to the far end of the square, away from the lights and the atmosphere, where there were spare hitching posts located under some spreading oak trees at the edge of the hilltop. It was a secluded spot that looked down over the pasture below.

"Will the horses be all right here?" Issie asked as she undid her girth, slid Amira's saddle off her back and slung it over the hitching rail.

"They will be fine," Francoise said. "This is a very organised event. There are grooms that come to check on all the horses every hour or so. They will provide hay nets and water as well."

As they walked back towards the town hall, Issie saw Francoise stiffen. There was a sullen expression on her face when Alfie pointed to the stairs and said, "I think your date is waiting for you!"

Miguel Vega was standing at the top of the steps in front of the main doors. He had dressed up for the occasion in the traditional *vaquero* attire of a *chaquetilla* – a short cropped jacket, and three-quarter length *vaquero* trousers, both of which made him look even shorter than he already was. His bright purple cummerbund was fighting valiantly to contain his rotund belly, but it was losing the battle and the buttons of his lilac frilled shirt were strained to the point of popping.

Vega took a lilac lace handkerchief out of his suit pocket and mopped his perspiring brow. Then he gave a broad grin and extended his hand to a horrified Francoise. "My date is here at last!" he said rather too gleefully.

Francoise blanched, but she had no choice but to take his hand, and they walked together through the front doors.

Issie took Alfie's hand too and they walked in together. The dance hall was even prettier on the inside, with more coloured lights and lanterns. The parquet wooden floors had been polished to a shine for dancing.

Issie and Alfie made a beeline for the punchbowl to get glasses of orange juice mixed with lemonade and ice. It was a yummy concoction.

"Do you want to dance to the next song?" Alfie asked Issie.

"Umm are they going to play any, you know, normal music?" Issie asked. "Or is it all going to be this old-fashioned stuff? Because I don't now how to waltz or anything like that..."

"Stop making excuses!" Alfie took the punch glass off her and put it down on the table, then grabbed her by the hand. "It's not that hard to learn. I'll show you!"

Alfie's dancing style wasn't exactly traditional. He flung Issie about on the dance floor as if they were in a particularly frenetic episode of *Strictly Come Dancing*.

"Alfie!" Issie had a bad case of the giggles as he dipped and twisted her so vigorously that she could hardly breathe. "Alfie stop it! People are looking!" The two of them were drawing grumpy stares from some of the older dancers, who were taking their own dance moves far more seriously and didn't approve of their comedy routine.

"Come on then," Alfie said, grinning and puffing with exertion from their antics. "Let's go sit down for a bit."

On the floor in front of them, Mrs Brown and Roberto were dancing up a storm.

"I didn't realise your mum was such a great dancer!" Alfie said to Issie.

"Neither did I!" Issie was amazed. Mrs Brown and Roberto were now doing an excellent *paso doble*, the bullfighters dance, across the centre of the room. Mrs Brown was clapping in time to the music and flicking her hands up like a professional, clearly having the time of her life.

"Our parents are better dancers than us," Alfie pulled a face.

"Maybe they're better at this sort of dancing," Issie reluctantly agreed, "but you should see my mum throwing shapes to my music – not such a pretty sight!"

Francoise, meanwhile, was also on the dance floor, with Miguel Vega. She had a face as sour as month-old milk, and instead of clapping and twisting to the *paso doble* she stood there with her hands on her hips looking thoroughly fed up while Vega danced avidly around her, clapping and stamping, thrusting his chin out and throwing his hands in the air.

The *paso doble* finally ended. The music changed tempo and the couples on the dance floor moved closer to each other. The men grabbed the women tightly around their waists and looked deep into their eyes.

"It's a tango," Alfie said. "The dance of love."

Issie watched as Roberto did a neat bow to Mrs Brown and then whispered something in her ear as she blushed.

Issie felt a stab of panic at this intimate gesture. Could it be that Stella had a point? Was her mum really falling in love with Roberto?

"*Madre mia*!" Alfie muttered, shaking Issie out of her thoughts. "Vega looks like he has Francoise in a headlock!"

Vega had the Frenchwoman in a vice-like grip, his chubby arms wrapped around her, as he tangoed her with great determination across the dance floor. As the music swelled, Vega seized the moment. He thrust Francoise backwards in a dramatic dip which took her by surprise and threw her off-balance. Then, as he pulled her back up again, ensnaring her even more tightly in his arms, he shut his eyes and leaned in for a kiss.

"Ohmygod!" Issie squeaked in horror, "I can't look!"

She peeked out between her fingers and saw that Vega had closed his eyes and lunged for the kiss, but his lips had missed their target. At the very last moment Francoise had been snatched roughly out of his arms and Vega was left puckering up into thin air. When he opened his eyes, there was a man standing in front of him where Francoise should have been.

"Arrghh!" Vega spat out. "What are you doing here?"

"I hope you don't mind," Tom Avery said. "I'm cutting in on this dance."

Vega's expression changed from amorous to angry. "Mind? Of course I do! Get your hands off my dance partner," he commanded.

"I'm afraid there's been a mistake," Avery told Vega.

"Francoise isn't your partner. She was meant to be here with me."

"She said yes when I asked her! You cannot turn up at a dance like this and take another man's partner!" Vega fumed.

"It should be Francoise's choice," Avery said, "so why don't we let the lady decide?"

He turned to her. "Francoise, I'm no good at romance. I've been a bachelor for so long," Avery admitted. "I always wanted to ask you to the dance but I left it too late…"

"Yes!" Vega interrupted him. "You left it too late! She is my partner now! Step aside…"

"Wait!" Avery cautioned Vega, "I'm not finished!" He turned back to Francoise. "I've been a fool, I know that – partly because you've pointed it out to me…" he smiled at her. "But I realised tonight that I couldn't bear the thought of another man with his arms around you on the dance floor. I love you, Francoise. Will you do me the honour of dancing with me?"

The whole room had stopped dancing. Everyone had heard Avery's declaration of love and they were waiting to hear Francoise's reply. She stood there in front of him, with tears in her eyes, lips trembling. Finally she spoke, "Tom, I…"

Suddenly the front doors to the hall flew open and one of the grooms raced inside the hall, panting and wild-eyed.

"Hurry! Please! Everybody!" he shouted. "It's the horses. They've been attacked!"

CHAPTER 12

There was a crush at the door as everybody panicked and tried to get outside all at once. In the rush, Issie and Alfie were both pushed to the very back of the crowd. By the time they got outside it was madness. There were people racing about everywhere, trying to recapture horses that had broken loose and were running free in the square.

"This way!" Alfie grabbed Issie by the hand and led her down a side path, staying close to the walls of the houses and out of the way of loose horses and the crowds. They ran towards the hitching posts where they had left their horses, beneath the trees at the far end of the square. Avery and Francoise were already there ahead of them. Issie could see Avery hanging on to a wild-eyed Victorioso and also trying to handle his own horse, Sorcerer, who was skipping beside him.

Francoise had Marius and was holding him tightly by his head collar.

"Where are the others?" Issie shouted out to Francoise. "Where are Amira and Aliya?"

Her question was answered a moment later when she heard the loud clarion call of a stallion and looked down the steep banks of the hill to the pasture below. In the moonlight she could see the two terrified liver chestnut mares. They were running with their ears flat back, and on either side, making it impossible for them to escape, were two stallions, the black and the dun. Leading the way across the pasture towards the gorge was a third stallion, dove grey, and even at a distance Issie could make out the strange two-tone black and white colours of his flying mane.

The bachelor stallions had staged yet another raid, and this time they had got away with not one but two of the El Caballo's best mares. They had taken Aliya and Amira.

Roberto wasted no time once he saw what had

happened. He took control of Marius and hastily threw on his saddle and cinched the girth. Alfie meanwhile, was preparing to mount Victorioso and Avery had Sorcerer saddled too, ready to go. Francoise looked anxious as he mounted up. "Please be careful, Tom. Those stallions are dangerous and unpredictable."

"Don't worry," Avery reassured her, "I'll be back soon."

Francoise smiled. "Stay safe," she insisted.

Issie had wanted desperately to ride after the bachelor stallions too, but she had no choice but to stay behind. Francoise agreed that it was awful being left without a horse as they watched the men gallop off down the hill without them. They stood there in the darkness watching the riders disappear from sight.

"Well," Mrs Brown said, "I'm not sure how well these shoes will cope with the walk home." She lifted her Spanish skirt and peered down at her pretty high heels. "They were made for dancing the tango, not trekking the countryside! But I suppose we'll have to give it a go."

The walk took less time than they had thought, and Mrs Brown's shoes survived intact. Once they were back at the hacienda, Mrs Brown went straight to the kitchen to put on a pot of strong coffee. They were only just sitting down with their mugs of latte in the front room when there was the sound of hoofbeats in the courtyard.

"They are back already!" Francoise said, looking out the window.

"Do they have the mares?" Issie asked.

"No," Francoise shook her head. "They are alone."

Outside in the courtyard, Roberto, Alfie and Avery were leading their horses back towards the stables.

"No sign of them?" Francoise asked as she came outside on to the steps of the hacienda.

"We gave up when we reached the other side of the gorge," Avery said. "They were long gone by then and it was too dark to follow them, so we rode straight back."

"We'll come and help you to unsaddle," Issie offered.

But Roberto shook his head. "It is late. Go to bed, Isadora, and leave it to us. There is nothing else you can do tonight."

Issie came downstairs to breakfast the next morning to find that Avery and Roberto were already gone again. Francoise, who was busily dishing up bacon and eggs, told her that they'd left before dawn to make one more search for the missing mares.

Despite the late-night dramas, Francoise also seemed determined that *haute école* training was to go ahead as normal. Issie finished breakfast and headed down to the stables to find Alfie saddling up one of the Andalusians ready to ride.

"You didn't go with your dad and Avery then?" Issie asked him.

"They didn't ask me!" Alfie looked annoyed. "They never mentioned it last night and they were gone by the time I woke up this morning."

"Maybe they knew you couldn't come because you had to train today?" Issie offered.

"Maybe," Alfie said. "Or maybe my father still thinks of me as a child. I don't suppose it helps that the last time he left me in charge of the herd Margarita was stolen!"

"That wasn't your fault," Issie insisted. "You know that those stallions can sniff out mares from miles away…"

Issie's heart began to race as a thought occurred to her. "Alfie, the stallions could smell the mares last time, couldn't they? So why don't we use more mares to lure them back again?"

"You mean use our horses as bait?" Alfie asked. "Dad would never allow it – we've lost three already!"

"But this time we'll be ready to follow the stallions when they take the mares! We'd track them down and get all the mares back again!" Issie insisted.

She took Angel by the reins and began to lead him down the stable corridor.

"Where are you going?" Alfie called after her. "We have training now!"

"I'm going to find those stallions," Issie replied. She looked back over her shoulder. "Are you coming with me?"

Alfie sighed in resignation and picked up the reins of his Andalusian stallion.

"*Madre mia*!" Alfie shook his head and followed Issie out into the cobbled courtyard. "I must be as crazy as you are!"

The two young riders left the gates of El Caballo a few minutes later. Issie was mounted up on Angel and leading a cobra of three of the stables' best mares. They were liver chestnut Arabians, just like Amira and Aliya, and Issie was convinced that these mares would prove to be an irresistible temptation to the bachelor stallions.

An hour later, however, Issie could feel her conviction ebbing away. They had brought the mares up through the gorge to the upper pastures and let them loose in the same spot where Margarita had been stolen. They had lain in wait behind a grove of trees and watched and waited. But the stallions had not come. It felt like they had been there forever, and there was still no sign of the bachelors.

"I'm sorry. It was a stupid plan," Issie said. She shifted about uncomfortably in her saddle and looked at the mares grazing peacefully. "Maybe we should give up. We can't sit here forever."

"No," Alfie disagreed. "They'll come. We just have

to wait…" He suddenly stopped speaking. They could both hear the sound of hoofbeats approaching!

A few moments later, around the bend of the hill, came the three bachelor stallions. As usual, the grey Sorraia was leading the herd. Behind, flanking him to the left and right, were the big black stallion and the dun. Issie hoped that the stallions might have Margarita, Aliya and Amira with them, but they were nowhere to be seen.

The mares that Issie had chosen as bait were all Anglo-Arabs like Amira and Aliya. They were liver chestnuts as well, with white socks, white blazes and the same pretty dished faces as their stable mates. Issie watched as the dun stallion circled the three mares, nipping at them and driving them towards the Sorraia. The grey Sorraia stallion made a vicious lunge at one of the mares, biting her hard on the neck so that the mare let out an angry squeal.

"He's hurting her!" Issie couldn't stand to watch.

"No!" Alfie hissed. "She'll be all right. He's just asserting his dominance – look!"

The mares were moving in a herd now, obeying the Sorraia. As she watched the stallions manoeuvring the mares, Issie was glad she had chosen to ride Angel this time. Nightstorm would never have been able to stand by and let the bachelor stallions steal the herd. He would have reacted the same way he had done last time, attacking and fighting back. But Angel was not like Nightstorm. He was a gentle stallion and his Iberian bloodlines made him calm and obedient. As long as Issie was on his back, he would do as she asked.

The Sorraia set off at a canter and, with the dun and the black stallion bringing up the rear, they herded the mares off around the curve of the hill.

"Wait until they are around the corner," Issie whispered to Alfie. "We don't want to let the stallions know we are here."

"And we don't want to lose them either!" Alfie was beginning to panic. "If they take another three mares my father will kill me."

"Come on then," Issie agreed. "Now!"

The two riders pressed their horses into a gallop and set off in the same direction as the stallions.

As they rounded the corner of the hill the horses were nowhere in sight.

"We have lost them!" Alfie groaned.

"No!" Issie shook her head. "Listen! I can hear them. They're just ahead of us."

The echo of hoofbeats was coming from the dirt path ahead that led off to the left. They followed the same route, keeping their horses at a steady gallop, trying to keep pace with the stallions.

A few minutes later the sound of hoofbeats became more distant and Issie began to worry that they had taken a wrong turn and lost them this time. She was even more concerned when rocky cliffs rose up around them and there was a fork in the narrow path as it split in two directions.

"Which way?" she asked Alfie.

He pulled his horse to a halt. "If we go to the right, that path will take us back down to the olive grove. To the left, there's a canyon; it's a dead-end."

As he said this, Angel raised his head and pricked his ears in the direction of the canyon and let out a whinny.

"He can hear something that we can't," Issie said. She pointed towards the dead-end canyon. "Come on, we're going this way."

"OK," Alfie said, "but take it slowly from here,

and let me go in front. If the stallions are in this canyon then they'll be corralled in by the canyon walls at that end. They may panic and try to get past us and I don't want to end up with another fight on our hands."

Issie agreed, and they cantered on in single file. As they rounded the bend, the canyon neck narrowed for a hundred metres or so, hemming them in, and then they emerged out the other side into an amphitheatre-like space, a dead-end canyon just as Alfie had said, with steep cliffs bordering it on every side. The rocky terrain was covered with trees and lantana bushes.

Alfie pointed beyond the lantana bushes. "Over there! Look!"

To the far right of the canyon Issie saw a horse moving and the dun stallion came into view. A moment later she spotted Margarita and Aliya. The mares were here too! Including Vega's Laeticia and the three new additions that the stallions had just taken. The mares were nervously greeting each other with snorts and snuffles while the stallions stood back, looking pleased with their new harem.

"OK," Issie whispered to Alfie. "So we've found them. Now what?"

"Issie," Alfie hissed back, "this was your plan, remember?"

"OK, OK," Issie said, "I know. Don't rush me!" She looked down at the stallions. "If we try and get all the mares out by ourselves now, we might lose them again."

Alfie nodded. "We need help."

"You go back to the hacienda," Issie told him. "Hopefully your dad and Avery will be back there by now. Get them and Francoise and some of the men. I'll stay here and keep watch, and make sure they don't go anywhere."

"OK," Alfie said. "Stay out of trouble. I'll be back as soon as I can."

He turned the Andalusian around and headed back towards the narrow mouth of the canyon. Issie watched him go, and then turned her attention back to the stallions and the mares.

The horses had moved away from the undergrowth to a patch of grassy flatland at the rear of the canyon. Most of the mares were grazing, but the three new mares still held their heads high and looked tense. It wasn't surprising, Issie thought. This morning they had been locked safely in their stalls at El Caballo Danza Magnifico. Now, here they were, being held hostage by a group of bachelor stallions.

Margarita seemed the most self-assured of the mares. She was definitely the alpha, the leader of the harem. She was also the mare that the Sorraia seemed the most interested in. Stallions often have favourite mares in a harem and it was clear that Margarita was the Sorraia's chosen one. It was also clear that Margarita didn't feel the same way about the Sorraia.

When the Sorraia trotted over to Margarita and began to try and affectionately groom her neck, the mare resisted, throwing up her head in defiance. The Sorraia grew angry at this. His authority in the herd was being threatened by this headstrong mare. He lunged at Margarita, his ears flattened back against his head as he tried to bite her hard on her neck. Margarita squealed and fought back, lashing out with her hind legs. The Sorraia dodged her hooves and came back at her again, plunging his teeth into the shoulder of the mare, this time drawing blood as he delivered a vicious bite. Margarita let out a heart-wrenching whinny as the stallion bit deep into her flesh, and then another squeal as he dealt her a blow with his front hooves, striking her hard on the same shoulder. The blow caused Margarita to lose her balance and fall. As the mare went down, Issie suddenly couldn't control herself any longer.

"No! Leave her alone!" Her voice rang out in the quiet of the canyon. The stallion stopped his attack on Margarita and looked in Issie's direction. She froze. But it was too late. The Sorraia had seen her.

"Uh-oh…" Issie's heart began to pound. The Sorraia still had his ears flat back and his eyes were filled with black hatred at the sight of the girl and the grey stallion. He was in battle mode, ready to strike. And Issie and Angel were his target.

CHAPTER 13

As the Sorraia bore down on them, teeth bared and ears flat back, Issie had only one thought. *Run.* She turned Angel and kicked him on, cantering back down the path between the trees and scrub, towards the narrow mouth of the canyon. Unfortunately the other stallions had also been alerted to her presence and the black stallion had already anticipated her next move. He had circled around the herd to the right and now stood guard in the neck of the canyon, blocking Issie's path.

Issie pulled Angel to a halt. Should they try and barge their way past the black horse? Issie took a good, hard look at the stallion, snorting and quivering, holding his ground in front of her, and she knew that it would be foolish to try and make a dash past him. There wasn't enough space to get through the narrow canyon neck, and if the black stallion attacked they would have no hope of getting out of his way. So they stayed trapped where they were – with a wild stallion blocking their exit, while another cantered up behind them, getting closer with every stride.

The Sorraia had Angel in his sights and his eyes shone with hatred. His ears were flat against his head, making him look almost demonic in his fury. Issie had to do something.

"Come on, Angel!" Issie took the only route left, riding away from both of the stallions, taking the rocky path through the lantana bushes that veered off to the right of the canyon interior. The path led nowhere. She would still be hemmed in by the dead-end of the high canyon walls where the mares were being held. But at least it bought some time and got her away from the Sorraia.

Angel was cantering, but he kept slipping and losing his footing. The path they were riding on was little more than a goat track and to get through Angel had to plough his way through the undergrowth and sprawling lantana bushes. There was no way to avoid the tangle of branches as they scratched and gouged at Issie's skin. Still, she figured it was better to get a few scratches than face a wild stallion!

The path through the bushes would take her and Angel all the way to the back of the canyon, circling behind the herd of mares. They could continue to avoid the stallions for a while this way, hiding in the undergrowth and sticking close to sheer cliff face of the canyon. Issie's goal was to try to reach the mares. Her plan was to mingle in amongst them, staying hidden from the stallions until Alfie returned.

Unfortunately the mares weren't so keen on her plan. Margarita was already on edge after being harassed and bullied by the Sorraia, so when Issie and Angel emerged from the lantana bushes and tried to ride up close to her Margarita put her ears back. As Angel brushed past her hindquarters the mare lashed out. Issie hadn't been expecting this and Margarita's flying hooves caught her off guard. The mare managed to clip Issie's leg with one of her hooves and Issie felt a sudden, searing jolt of pain in her calf.

For a moment the pain made everything go black. Issie looked down at her leg. There was a rip in her jods and blood was soaking into the fabric, but she didn't think her leg was badly injured. She knew now though that she mustn't get too close to the mares.

Making sure to stay away from Margarita's hindquarters this time, Issie rode Angel in amongst the herd, weaving between Aliya and Amira, trying to stay near but making sure that she didn't spook the mares or prompt them to lash out. The kick to her leg had been incredibly painful, but she didn't have time to think about it. Her main concern was getting past the stallions and out of the canyon. A fully-fledged attack by a stallion could do much worse damage.

Stallions like these, young bachelors with something to prove and a harem of mares to protect, were dangerous. She remembered what Avery had said about how they often postured and bullied each other, rather then getting involved in a real fight. But she also remembered his final words – *occasionally their fights can become lethal, and when humans are involved or their herd is under threat then yes, they will go on the attack and may kill.*

Issie was again relieved that she hadn't chosen to ride Storm today. Angel, thankfully, had an unbelievably docile nature for a stallion. He was a true Andalusian horse, and the breed was famed for its quiet, even temperament. Angel would do whatever Issie told him to do. And right now all Issie wanted to do was escape.

Issie had been aware for some time that the Sorraia stallion was closing in on her. He'd followed Issie and Angel on their path through the lantana bushes and in amongst the harem of mares. It was getting impossible for Issie to keep mares between her and the Sorraia, so she retreated and trotted in a wide loop around the herd to end up at the back of the canyon once more. Unable to go any further, with Angel's rump against the cliff face, Issie urged her horse to move sideways away from the Sorraia. Angel responded, crossing his legs neatly in a half-pass, but the manoeuvre was only taking them straight back into the lantana bushes where they had started a few minutes ago. Issie's skin was getting scratched to bits on the dense thickets as she was pressed back further into the canyon by the Sorraia.

Riding past a large lantana bush, she seized the opportunity to reach out and grab a thick stick, snapping it off and wrenching it loose. It was about the size and length of a dressage whip. Not much in the way of protection against three wild stallions, but at least it was a weapon of sorts. She gripped on to the stick and kept Angel side-stepping further along the canyon wall. The Sorraia was only a few metres away now, preparing to attack. The stallion sounded his clarion call once more. Issie knew she had run out of time. They had to go now! She urged Angel on and expected him to gallop forward. But the stallion gave a surprised snort and reared up instead!

"Angel!" Issie shrieked and flung herself forward, gripping the grey stallion's silky mane to hang on.

Startled by his rider, Angel promptly put all four feet back on the ground. And then Issie realised that Angel hadn't been rearing at all. He had simply been doing exactly what he thought Issie had asked of him – he had been performing a levade!

Issie must have mistakenly cued the stallion by tapping him with the lantana stick. The skinny branch in her hand might prove to be a greater weapon than she could have possibly anticipated. What if she were to use it as a dressage whip? She remembered what Avery had told her about the *haute école*, how the origins of the movements came from the battlefield. They were war manoeuvres!

OK, so the bachelor stallions were not your typical enemy, but hadn't Avery said that rearing and attack stances were often enough to defuse a fight between stallions? The skills that she had learnt in the dressage arena might be enough to intimidate them. If she could make Angel look like he was on the attack, would that be enough to warn the Sorraia off?

The Sorraia was circling back to strike again. Issie had to act. She tried to focus, gathering up her reins and sitting up straight in the saddle. Issie shook the negative thoughts out of her head. This time she couldn't afford to mess up. Her life and Angel's depended on it.

Gingerly, Issie gave Angel his cue, tapping his shoulder. The grey stallion rose up balanced on his hindquarters and, instead of shrieking Issie sat perfectly still, at one with her horse. Then, with a deft flick of the stick, she tapped Angel on his flank in just the right spot. The Andalusian stallion gathered all his power in his hind legs and then leapt forward balancing on his hindquarters in a perfect courbette!

The *haute école* movement had exactly the effect that Issie hoped it would. The Sorraia was suddenly dwarfed by the Andalusian towering above him. As Angel leapt towards him in enormous bounds, the Sorraia was totally outclassed. He began to retreat as Angel leapt onwards, spurred on by Issie's rhythmical whip taps on his flank.

Angel was almost clear of the lantana scrub when he suddenly lost his footing on the rocky ground and came crashing back down to earth on all fours once more. It was enough though. The courbette had worked. The Sorraia had been thoroughly intimidated by Angel's physical power and size and had retreated back in amongst the mares.

The dun stallion, however, had now become a threat. He was moving in fast to launch his own attack on Angel. He had circled the mares and was coming at them from the rear, his teeth bared.

The dun stallion was only a few metres away when Issie saw him out of the corner of her eye. She reacted on pure adrenalin, preparing her horse with lightning speed. Once again she urged Angel back up into a levade. She held Angel there for just a moment, until the dun stallion was so close that he was about to strike.

"Now!" Issie shouted. And with a quick, deft flick of the stick she touched Angel's rump and he leapt up into the air. Angel flew out like a gazelle with all four legs off the ground. He seemed to freeze in mid-air as Issie reached back and gave the crucial tap in just the right spot on his hind legs. The grey stallion took his cue and lashed out, thrusting both hind legs in a balletic kick. Angel managed to land both his hind hooves squarely on the chest of the dun stallion, connecting while he was still in mid-air. The dun was sent reeling by the unexpected blow. He fell to the ground, landing hard on his side, legs akimbo.

Issie was horrified. She had only been trying to protect herself, but what if she had actually hurt the dun? She held her breath and then felt utter relief when the horse got up to his feet, clearly stunned but not seriously harmed.

Preoccupied by her concern for the dun, Issie never saw the black stallion coming at her. The black horse struck swiftly and violently, rearing up over Angel bringing the full force of his front legs down on the grey stallion's left shoulder. The unexpected blow from the black horse sent Angel reeling. He fell to the ground, landing flat on his side. As he went down, Issie flew out of the saddle.

When you are falling off a horse and you know the

impact is about to come, you try to prepare yourself for the crash. Issie was practised at it and knew how to tumble-roll to absorb the shock. But this time she wasn't prepared at all. She hit the ground badly, landing hard on her side, the wind completely knocked out of her. She was gasping for breath, and shaking with panic. Angel was lying beside her on the ground and there was a deep cut in his shoulder where the hooves of the black horse had struck him.

"Angel?" Issie's vision was blurred by grit and tears. "Angel!" She dragged herself through the dust to the grey stallion's side. "Angel!" Issie shook the stallion with both hands. "Get up! I need you!"

On the ground, without Angel to defend her, she was totally vulnerable. A single blow of a stallion's hoof could be deadly.

Issie looked around wildly. Where was Alfie? Issie desperately wished he was here. She needed help now! Angel wasn't getting up and Issie was still feeling winded and finding it hard to breathe.

The black stallion meanwhile, was about to move in on Issie and Angel to strike again.

"Angel!" Issie tried to rally the horse once more,

"Angel! Come on, get up! You have to get up. Please…"

The sudden sound of galloping hoofbeats entering the canyon seemed to come out of nowhere. It must be Alfie! He was back after all!

"Alfie! I'm over here!" Issie called out.

But no reply came. And then Issie heard the familiar whinny, and she knew who it was. Help had come at last, but not Alfie or the riders of El Caballo. She looked up at the narrow neck of the canyon and the sight of the dapple-grey gelding galloping towards her made her heart soar. It was her horse.

It was Mystic.

CHAPTER 14

A moment ago the black stallion had been ready to attack, but the sight of Mystic drew his attention away from Issie and Angel. The stallion focused on this new horse, wondering what kind of a threat this latest intruder might be to his harem.

This was Issie's chance and she seized it. "Come on, Angel, ughhhh!" She grabbed the grey stallion by his bridle and pulled as hard as she could, trying one last time to force him to stand up.

The blow he had taken must have almost knocked Angel out. Snorting and quivering, the grey horse propped himself up on his front legs and then, with enormous effort, and the help of Issie's encouragingly vigorous tugs on his reins, the Andalusian stallion stumbled to his feet again.

"Good boy, Angel!" Issie was so relieved. He was wobbly, but at least he was standing. They needed to get out of there. Mystic couldn't possibly keep all three stallions away from them forever.

Issie had expected the grey gelding to come for her, but instead Mystic headed towards the mares. She saw him galloping and darting through the lantana bushes with the black stallion and the Sorraia both following. Mystic was circling back around the harem, trying to encourage the mares to move, flicking his head and nickering as he cantered around them.

Issie understood what he was trying to do. If Mystic could get the mares to stampede towards the canyon neck then the three bachelor stallions would have no choice but to follow them, and they would leave Issie and Angel alone.

Margarita was the first mare to dart towards the canyon mouth. The grey gelding was offering her a chance to escape and she took it. As Mystic drove the mares from behind, she led them from the front. As Margarita began to canter in the right direction the mares willingly followed her. It didn't take much urging from Mystic to get them into a gallop and the herd moved in unison, heading for the exit.

The bachelor stallions tried to stop the mares, cantering alongside them, trying to nip and cajole them back again. But Margarita fought back! She bared her teeth and lunged at the black stallion when he came near her, warning him off. Then she led the mares on with Mystic behind them galloping towards freedom.

Freedom, Issie thought. If the mares made it away from the stallions and out of the canyon then they would be on their own and Issie might never find them again. Still, it was better for the mares to roam wild than be trapped here by the stallions. Not that Issie had much choice in the matter. Right now, with Angel badly wounded, her only thoughts had to be for herself and her stallion. They had to get out of here themselves and get back to the hacienda. They couldn't risk staying here any longer when the stallions might return and attack again.

Issie bent down to look at Angel's wounded shoulder. Blood was still oozing from the cut where the black stallion's hooves had struck, but it was a clean wound, and not too deep. She stepped the horse forward. He was lame all right, but he could walk. They could get out of here, but it would be a slow walk home.

Issie was just thinking this when the sound of hoofbeats began thundering towards her through the canyon again, getting closer, louder.

Terrified, she began to lead the stallion back towards the lantana bushes. Issie didn't know what else to do. They couldn't run, but perhaps they could hide…

"Isadora!" She heard Alfie shouting above the sound of the hoofbeats, "Issie! Are you OK?"

The sight of Alfie and Avery riding towards her made Issie literally weep with relief. "Ohmygod, Alfie!" she shouted back. "I thought you were the wild stallions!"

Alfie shook his head. "We passed them at the other end of the canyon. They scattered when they saw us. Roberto and Francoise managed to corral the mares. They're leading them back to the hacienda. We came here looking for you."

Avery, meanwhile, had flung himself down off Sorcerer's back even before the horse had come to a stop and raced over to Issie. "Are you all right?" he asked, looking at Issie's tear-stained face and the wound on her leg. "Are you hurt?"

Issie wiped her face with her sleeve and nodded, "I'm all right now, Tom." Then she managed a smile. "You should have been here a few minutes ago," she told him. "Angel did a perfect capriole!"

When Issie walked in through the gates of El Caballo Danza Magnifico leading the battered and bloodied Angel beside her, the first thing she saw was her mother sprinting across the courtyard. Mrs Brown flung her arms around her in a hug that was so tight Issie couldn't breathe.

"Thank goodness you're safe!" Mrs Brown had clearly been quite beside herself with worry. "When Alfie came back without you and said you were out there on your own with those stallions I began to think the worst had happened…"

"I'm OK, Mum, don't worry," said Issie.

Mrs Brown finally loosened her grip on her daughter and stood back to take a good look at her. "You're filthy!" she exclaimed. "And you're covered in blood!"

"Most of it's Angel's blood, Mum," Issie said. "I've just got a cut on my leg, that's all."

"She got kicked by one of the mares and she's had a bit of a fright and a bad fall," Avery said.

"Tom!" Issie turned and pulled a face at her instructor for telling on her. "Honestly, the fall was fine," Issie explained, "it was just the landing that sucked!"

"We should get a doctor to look at your leg." Mrs Brown sounded really worried.

Issie turned to Avery, "We should get a vet to look at Angel's shoulder too."

The vet arrived late that afternoon and put six stitches in the wound on Angel's shoulder. While Roberto and Francoise watched, Issie held the lead rope of the big, grey Andalusian as the vet gave him a sedative to numb the pain. She gently stroked the stallion's face as the stitches were swabbed and a salve put on the wound. The scar left behind was in the shape of a horse shoe. Issie had been right though – the wound wasn't deep and the vet said that Angel would be ready to ride in the dressage school again by the end of the week.

Issie stayed in the stall with Angel and Francoise while Roberto saw the vet to the gates. "How are you feeling, boy?" Issie asked Angel after they'd gone. Angel nickered softly and nudged her with his velvety muzzle as if to say, "Don't worry, I'm OK."

"The sedative will wear off soon and you can feed him dinner if you like," Francoise told Issie when she returned. "And you heard what the vet said – by Thursday you can ride him in the school again."

"It's so weird," Issie said. "Last week I would have been celebrating if the vet told me I could have a few days off from dressage training. Now, it's the opposite. I can't wait to try a capriole again!"

The fight with the stallions had changed Issie's views forever about the *haute école*. It was no longer some outdated art. It was a living, breathing powerful weapon. Now that the awfulness of her clash in the canyon was over, Issie realised that she'd never experienced anything quite as amazing as the moment when Angel leapt into the air and performed a stunning capriole that floored his opponent with a quick thrust of his hindquarters.

Issie was awestruck that she was capable of unleashing

such power in her horse. She also felt terrible though, worrying about the dun stallion. What if they had really hurt him?

"You were fighting for your life," Francoise had reasoned with her. "You didn't have time to assess whether you would hurt the horse you were fighting against. Besides, when we arrived at the canyon all three stallions were galloping with the mares. The dun seemed perfectly fine."

Avery, Roberto and Alfie confirmed Francoise's story at dinner. But strangely, no one made any mention of Mystic. Was the dappled-grey still with the herd when they had recaptured the mares, or had he simply disappeared before the others arrived? Surely if he had still been there following the harem then someone would have seen him?

Issie didn't question it too much. All she knew was that Mystic had been there when she had needed him the most. If Mystic hadn't arrived when the black stallion was about to attack her and Angel… well, she didn't like to think too hard about what might have happened.

Mrs Brown was still in overprotective-mother mode the next day. So when Issie insisted that she was well enough to go riding again on Storm, her mother decided that there was nothing else for it and insisted on coming with her.

Issie was stunned. She had spent so many years trying to convince her mother to come riding with her. "If I'd known that all I had to do was have a horseback fight with three wild stallions to get you to ride with me," Issie joked, "then I would have done it sooner!"

As they saddled up together Issie helped her mum to tighten the girth and adjust the stirrups on Ferdinand's saddle. The chubby chestnut pony dozed in the afternoon sun as Issie did up the straps on his bridle. "He looks a bit frisky," Mrs Brown said dubiously.

"Mum!" Issie giggled. "He's a twenty-three-year-old bomb-proof Spanish pony. He's about as frisky as a garden snail!"

Once she'd made sure that Mrs Brown was ready and mounted up, Issie unlocked the top door of Angel's stall to check on him before they left. She was pleased to see that the stallion was standing quite comfortably, happily munching his way through the last scraps of his hay net.

"You were super brave out there yesterday," she told the stallion. "You beat the Sorraia, you know that, don't you? It was three against one, and you managed to hold them off until help arrived." She gave Angel a loving stroke down his velvety nose and her fingers ran over the lumps and bumps of the stallion's *serreta* scars. They were like a map of his life experiences – and now there was a new scar forming. The wound inflicted by the black stallion was healing and very soon only a thin line would be left behind, almost like a brand on Angel's shoulder. "It's the mark of the *haute école*," Issie murmured to the stallion. She knew that whenever she saw that scar she would remember how they had used their dressage skills on the battlefield against three wild stallions and lived to tell the tale.

Issie emerged from Angel's stall to find Mrs Brown wrestling with Ferdinand, who was helping himself to the hay bales stacked on one side of the corridor.

"Thank heavens you're back! I was petrified that he would bolt while you were gone," Mrs Brown said.

"Bolt?" Issie giggled. "Mum, you'll be lucky if you can get him to move after all the hay you've let him scoff!"

Nightstorm was already tacked up to go. When Issie brought him out into the corridor and mounted up she noticed that her mother was giving her a rather odd look.

"I was just thinking," Mrs Brown said, "how grown-up you look on that horse of yours."

Issie rode over to her mother and Ferdinand. "I'm taller than you!" she grinned. It was true – sitting on her sixteen-three stallion, Issie positively towered over her mother and the stocky little Ferdinand!

"Would you like me to put a lead rein on Ferdy," she offered with a straight face, "or do you think you can manage on your own?"

"I'm fine, thank you," Mrs Brown said sniffily. And then she added. "But no trotting! I still haven't figured out how to do that rising thing!"

Once they were outside the gates of El Caballo's compound and on the soft, dirt track that ran through the fields, Issie decided that the time had finally come to get her mother trotting properly.

"Rising trot is easy," she insisted. "All you do is go up when the pony throws you up."

Mrs Brown shrieked and wobbled at first as Ferdinand

set off at a trot, but with Issie right there beside her explaining how to use the stirrups to rise up with each bump, Mrs Brown began to give it a try, doing a few shaky rises in the saddle.

"That's it! Don't try too hard. Let the horse lift you out of the saddle and then down again... and up... and down... and up..."

It wasn't long before Mrs Brown was posting up and down with ease.

"This is fun!" she laughed.

"That's what I've been trying to tell you for years!" Issie rolled her eyes.

"All right," said Mrs Brown, already out of breath. "I think we can walk again now! That's enough rising trot for one day."

They took the long path today, the one that led down through the olive grove to a little orchard filled with pomegranate trees. Mrs Brown was talking on and on about pomegranates and ingredients for Spanish recipes and how Roberto had taught her to make a salad that required some strange and exotic Spanish oil that she would never be able to buy at home in Chevalier Point, and Issie suddenly noticed how much her mum's face lit up as she spoke about Spain and Roberto.

Ever since the dance Issie had been wondering whether Stella was right about her mum and Roberto.

Issie had to admit that when Stella first made the suggestion, she was horrified. For nearly seven years it had just been the two of them – Issie and her mum – and she liked their life in Chevalier Point. She didn't want anything to change. But as she listened to her mum gaily discussing paella and fiestas, Issie felt selfish. Her mum deserved to be happy too.

"Mum?" Issie said. "I want to tell you something."

"What is it, sweetie?" Mrs Brown smiled at her.

"It's about you and Roberto," Issie said. "I just want to say that I'm… I'm really happy for you. I mean that you're in love and all that…"

"Oh, Issie…" Mrs Brown began, but Issie interrupted her.

"No, let me finish, Mum. You've always looked after me and done so much for me and I know how hard you've worked so that I could have everything I wanted. And I'm almost sixteen, so I'm grown-up now. It's time that you started thinking about yourself. So if it really makes you happy being here in Spain with Roberto, then I'm OK with that…"

"Now, wait a minute," Mrs Brown said gently. "Listen, Issie…"

But Issie wouldn't be stopped. She took a deep breath. "Just tell me the truth, Mum. Are you going to marry Roberto? Are we moving to Spain?"

CHAPTER 15

The bells of the church in the village square rang out at ten every Sunday morning to call the villagers to morning service. But today was Thursday, and late in the afternoon the bells began their chorus, letting the village know that something special was about to happen.

Issie heard the bells ringing and a tingle ran up her spine. *It was time.*

She walked across her bedroom over to the full-length mirror and took one last look at her outfit. She straightened the straps on her dress and smoothed down the full skirt of the pink, lace gown. It was a bit too girly for her tastes, but then bridesmaid's dresses were always frilly, weren't they? She remembered an atrocious mauve gown that Stella had had to wear when she was her cousin's bridesmaid back in Chevalier Point – at least this dress was prettier than that monstrosity!

The church bells were ringing even louder now, and they sounded so joyful. Issie walked out to the balcony of her room and stood there with her eyes closed, listening to their chimes.

"Hey, you, up there on the balcony!" Issie looked down and saw Alfie smiling at her.

"Come on down!" Alfie said. "I've got Nightstorm ready for you." He was sitting on top of Victorioso and he was leading Nightstorm, the reins held lightly in his hand.

"Any sign of the bride and groom yet?" Issie asked.

Alfie shook his head. "You know what weddings are like. The bride never shows up until the last minute!"

The bridal party was supposed to be gathering together in the cobbled courtyard now and preparing to leave the Nunez hacienda to make the ride up the hillside to the church. The wedding service was due to begin at three.

Issie still couldn't believe any of this was actually happening. She was about to be a bridesmaid and witness two of the people she loved the most in the world getting married. Their lives were about to change forever.

"I'm coming!" she told Alfie.

As she raced for the front door, she stopped to grab the bunch of bridesmaid's flowers sat waiting for her on a chair in the hallway. The bouquet was made up of orange blossom and pink roses to match her gown. *At least*, Issie thought, *I don't have to carry the ring*. That was Alfie's job as the best man. Let him have the responsibility for that!

"Wow!" Alfie gave a low wolf whistle as Issie stepped out of the door. "You look beautiful."

"Thanks!" Issie smiled. "You don't look too bad yourself!"

Alfie was dressed in a black suit with a white shirt and black bow tie. The effect of his outfit was enhanced by the fact that he was mounted up on Victorioso – a jet-black stallion with white roses braided into his mane.

Standing beside Victorioso, Nightstorm had roses braided into his mane too, but his were pink to match Issie's dress.

"Storm ate two of the roses out of Victorioso's mane when my back was turned," Alfie complained as he passed Issie the reins. "I had to stick some more in. I hope they don't fall out in the middle of the wedding." "Well, it is a horseback wedding. Anything could happen," Issie giggled.

Alfie looked at his watch. "They're late." He was beginning to look nervous.

"Maybe, we should go and—"

Alfie was interrupted by the clatter of hooves on the cobbles of the courtyard, announcing the arrival of the rest of the wedding party.

Issie looked up and the first thing she saw was Angel. The grey stallion looked more beautiful than ever before. His long, silken mane flowed loose over his shoulders and had been threaded with silver ribbons that fell almost to the ground. His beautiful coat, the colour of creamy white parchment, was matched almost perfectly to the pale shade of the billowing, silk organza gown that the bride wore as she sat on his back. The skirts of the bride's dress fell in frothy layers, completely covering the saddle and quite a lot of the stallion as well. The train of the dress draped all the way over Angel's rump and tail, sweeping the ground. It was like something out of a fairytale. She was the most beautiful bride Issie had ever seen. An antique, lace veil covered her face, but the bride now lifted this back. She was smiling, her face radiating pure joy.

"Ohmygod!" Issie's eyes welled with tears. "I can't believe it! In just a few minutes you're going to be getting married! This is so incredible."

"*Oui*! I know!" Francoise D'arth said as she arranged her veil. Then she looked about smiling nervously. "Where is my husband-to-be?"

There was the sound of hooves on the cobblestones again and Roberto Nunez rode into view. Mrs Brown rode alongside him on Ferdinand, dressed as the maid of honour in a pink dress similar to Isadora's and a broad-brimmed pink hat.

"Your groom left twenty minutes ago for the chapel," Roberto reassured Francoise. "He will be there waiting for you."

Looking back now, Issie felt more than a bit silly about what she'd said to her mum on their ride together. Although, to be fair it wasn't all her fault. Stella was to blame as well! When Issie had summoned up the courage and asked Mrs Brown if she was going to marry Roberto, the response was certainly not what she had expected.

Mrs Brown had begun laughing so hard she had nearly fallen off her horse. "What an outlandish conclusion to jump to!" she hooted as Issie turned bright pink with embarrassment. "Of course I enjoy Roberto's company. It's been lovely having someone my own age to talk to and swap recipes with. But how did you get it into your head that I was about to up sticks and move to Spain with him?"

"Well, Stella said…" Issie began.

"Oh, I see!" Mrs Brown grinned. "I should have known that Stella would have something to do with this!"

"It wasn't just Stella!" Issie defended her friend. "You seemed to get on so well with Roberto, and you both like paella…"

"Mutual liking of paella is not a sign of true love! And it is certainly no reason to get married!" Mrs Brown laughed. Then she looked more serious. "Isadora, I'm not planning on marrying Roberto. We're just friends."

Issie had felt foolish, but her Mum made her feel much better when she added, "Sweetie, I would never change our lives so drastically or even think about getting involved with someone without talking it over with you first. Maybe one day I will meet someone special and want to get married again. But I'm in no hurry. I'm very happy with my life as it is, just you and me. In fact, I'm looking forward to getting home again. I love Andalusia, but I'm beginning to miss Chevalier Point!"

Issie smiled. "Me too."

Mrs Brown laughed, "And I'm going to give that Stella a piece of my mind as soon as we get back!"

Issie had been wrong about her mother and Roberto, but she hadn't failed to notice the change in the mood at the Nunez hacienda since the night of the harvest dance. When Avery had finally summoned up the courage on the dance floor to tell Francoise how he truly felt about her, Francoise hadn't had the chance to reply. But afterwards, when the couple were reunited, they admitted to each other for the first time that they really were in love.

"It was the most romantic moment of my life," Francoise told Issie later. "We went out riding together.

Tom had bought me a diamond engagement ring, and he hid it in a jewel box and hung it from an orange tree in the grove just outside the hacienda. As we rode past it, he pointed out the jewel box in amongst the boughs. I picked it from the branches and opened it up, and when I turned around he was already down off his horse and on one knee asking me to marry him!"

Francoise had said yes, of course, and the couple had been inseparable ever since. And now, just one week later, the church bells were ringing as the bridal party from the hacienda Nunez rode up the hill towards the pretty little stone chapel at the furthest end of the village.

As they rode along the cobbled streets in between the white houses of the village, women waved from their balconies and threw roses. Children raced after them, squealing and giggling as they ran alongside the horses, following the wedding party down the street, staring at the bride in her beautiful white gown.

"She looks amazing, doesn't she?" Mrs Brown said admiringly.

"She looks really happy," Issie said.

The service that day was held outside the church so that the bride and groom could remain on horseback the whole time. The minister in charge of proceedings wore white and gold robes and rode a mule.

"We are here today," the minister told the assembled guests, "to celebrate the marriage of Tom Avery and Francoise D'arth. If there is anyone here among us who objects to this union, let them speak now or forever hold their peace."

The loud clarion call of a stallion's cry rang out.

"Nightstorm!" Issie shushed her horse. "Be quiet!"

Everyone laughed. Thankfully there were no further interruptions.

"Tom Avery," the minister continued. "Do you take Francoise D'arth to be your lawfully wedded wife? Will you love, honour and cherish her, make sure you muck out her horse's stall before your own and keep the hard feed bins clean, for the rest of your life?"

"I will," Avery said.

"And you, Francoise D'arth," the minister continued, "will you love, honour and cherish Tom, promise never to use his favourite Pessoa saddle and leave the stirrups on the wrong holes, or clean the horse tack in the kitchen sink, forever and ever?"

"*Oui!* I will!" Francoise was smiling and there were

tears of joy in her eyes.

Issie vaulted down off Nightstorm and held Francoise and Avery's horses by the reins as the happy couple joined hands.

"Who has the rings?" The minister asked.

Alfie rode forward on Victorioso and handed the wedding bands to Tom and Francoise.

The minister watched as the rings were exchanged. "Tom Avery and Francoise D'arth," he said, "I now pronounce you man and wife. You may kiss the bride!"

There wasn't a dry eye among the assembled crowd when Avery leant over on his horse and his lips touched Francoise's. And then, in a shower of white roses and confetti, the bride and groom led the procession as the wedding party rode back home with the church bells ringing in their ears.

CHAPTER 16

The celebrations back at the hacienda lasted late into the night. Roberto had invited all the stable hands and the *jinetes,* and many of the villagers were there too. The party was well underway and Issie was at the buffet fetching a platter of sweet almond cakes when Miguel Vega walked through the door. An uncomfortable silence struck the room and all eyes turned to Vega as he strode across towards Francoise and Avery in the middle of the dance floor.

Vega stood in front of the newlyweds. Issie could see he had something in his hands. It was a silver box. "I have brought you a wedding gift," he said gruffly, thrusting it into Francoise's hands. "It is a toaster," he added. "I believe this is traditional, no?"

Francoise took the box and smiled, "Thank you, Miguel."

He turned to Avery now. "Congratulations on your wedding," he said grudgingly. "You are a very lucky man to have such a beautiful bride."

He extended his hand and Avery shook it.

Issie was still staring at this when Vega caught her eye and walked over towards her. "Little Chica!" he said. "I want to talk to you!"

Vega's face furrowed into a frown and Issie could see beads of sweat on his forehead. He pulled out his pocket handkerchief and dabbed at his face before he spoke. "I am told that I owe you a debt of gratitude," Vega said reluctantly. "They say that you are the one responsible for getting my Laeticia back from the bachelor stallions."

Alfie had raced to Issie's aid when he saw Vega approach her, but by the time he arrived at her side Vega was already taking his leave. Issie was wide-eyed with shock! Had Vega really just thanked her?

A moment later Roberto Nunez confirmed this. "I've just spoken to Miguel and he praised Isadora's efforts in getting Laeticia back," Roberto said. "He's also agreed to organise his men and help us to try and catch the stallions."

Over the past week there had been sightings of the three stallions, but no one had even come close to corralling them.

"They are still out there somewhere in the hills," Roberto said. "I am certain of it. But if they try again to take our mares, we will have men ready and hopefully we might track them down. It is not easy to catch a bachelor..." he grinned as he watched the bride and groom take to the dance floor for the wedding waltz, "... although it would seem that Francoise has managed the feat quite neatly!"

It had been a whirlwind of planning and preparations that week for the wedding, but now that Avery and Francoise were actually married Issie wondered what would happen next. Would her trainer move to Spain permanently to be with his bride?

It turned out that Issie had nothing to worry about, as she discovered when the future of the happy couple was revealed during the groom's speech at the wedding dinner that evening.

"My new wife has made me the happiest man in the world," Avery told the guests, "and she's going to be making the eventing riders of New Zealand very happy too... because she will be coming home with me to take up her new role as the head of dressage at Dulmoth Park."

Issie was thrilled with the news. "Now that you're coming back with us, you can continue Nightstorm's dressage training!" Issie told Francoise excitedly.

"Isadora," Francoise said, "I will be only too happy to help you train, but you are the one who will be in charge of your stallion's schooling. You have learnt well in your time in the riding school with the *jinetes*. You proved that in your fight against the stallions. You are a true master of the *haute école*."

It was clear that the *jinetes* agreed with her, for on the table along with the wedding presents there was a gift for Isadora. Jean-Jacques presented it to her and the rest of the *jinetes* stood by as she opened it. It was a polo shirt marked with the El Caballo crest – the letter C with a heart inscribed inside it.

"Only true El Caballo riders have the right to wear the uniform," Jean-Jacques said. "You have earned this. You are one of us now."

"Thank you," Issie was touched. "For everything."

Issie had always thought that dressage was the most

boring part of being an eventer, but not any more. "If I hadn't known those battle manoeuvres in the canyon that day, Angel and I would never have survived," she admitted to Francoise.

OK, maybe there wouldn't be any stallions to fight in her next competition, but she understood now that dressage was all about harnessing the incredible power of the horse – mastering its movements so you could achieve perfection together as horse and rider.

When she expressed this to Roberto, he nodded sagely. "At last you understand what I was trying to tell you," he said. "Dressage is the basis of everything we do. What good is power without control?"

"I get that now, I really do," Issie agreed.

"Then you are ready to take the Little One home," Roberto said, smiling, "and I wish you both well."

There were many more speeches about the bride and groom, and when it was Roberto's turn he paid tribute to Francoise. "She has been my head trainer at El Caballo Danza Magnifico for ten years now," Roberto told the guests. "It pains me very much to lose a great trainer and a great friend, but I am glad that she has found such happiness with the man I am proud to call my best friend, Tom Avery." Roberto took a moment to compose himself before he continued.

"Many people have asked me how I will ever replace such a brilliant head trainer. And I am very lucky that I have someone who has proven his skill and expertise and is now ready to take over the reins at my side at El Caballo Danza Magnifico…" Roberto raised his glass in a toast. "I would like you all to drink to the appointment of my new head trainer – my son, Alfonso Nunez!"

There was much hooting and cheering from the *jinetes* at this news. Alfie, who had no idea that his father had planned to give him the job as head trainer, looked completely stunned.

"I told your father that you were the perfect choice for the job," Francoise said as she gave Alfie a hug. "You are a brilliant trainer, Alfie, and, with you in charge, the horses and the *jinetes* will be in good hands."

The speeches were over – or at least so Francoise thought – but then Roberto cleared his throat once more and tapped on his crystal sherry glass to get the attention of the room. "I see that you have all left wedding presents on the table for the bride and groom," he told the crowd. "However, I have a special gift for the bride that is much too large to leave on the table. I would like to give it to her now."

As he said this, Jean-Jacques appeared with Francoise's wedding present. He was leading Angel, who wore a giant silver bow tied around his saddle.

"You are giving Angel to me?" Francoise could not believe it. "But Roberto! He is one of your very best stallions."

"And you will take the very best care of him – he will be happy with you," said Roberto, smiling. "Besides, who else can ride him here? You know he will not let a man on his back."

"He is a great stallion," Roberto went on. "Perhaps one day we may see more colts and fillies with his famous El Caballo bloodlines filling the fields of Chevalier Point."

"Thank you, Roberto," said Francoise, her eyes filling with tears.

Issie was overwhelmed too. They had come here to bring Storm home and now Angel would be returning to Chevalier Point as well!

"I may come and visit you soon," Alfie told her. "We are preparing once more for a world tour with the horses and we shall put Chevalier Point on the itinerary."

Farewells were so much easier when you knew you were going to see each other again.

"It's crazy," Issie told her mum. "A week ago I thought you were going to end up staying in Spain with Roberto. Now, it seems like we're taking half of Spain home with us instead!"

Plans had been made for the horse transporter to pick up Angel and Storm on Sunday morning. And so, on Saturday evening, when Roberto suggested that they all take one last ride together around the farm, everyone agreed. Even Mrs Brown was keen to have a last ride on Ferdinand.

"I shall miss him," she admitted, patting the chubby chestnut pony on his wide rump.

"Don't worry Mrs B.," Avery reassured her, "I have a couple of bomb-proof ponies at Dulmoth Park that would be perfect for you."

Issie led the way on Storm and the six riders rode in single file around the dusty path that led down past the olive grove and through the hills. The sun was shining brightly, and at one point Issie looked up to the horizon ahead and saw the glimmering outline of a horse against the skyline. She was certain it was Mystic, silhouetted against the Spanish sun. It was as if he was checking up on Issie and Storm one last time. Then, with a flick of his mane, the grey pony cantered off and was gone.

Nightstorm raised his head in the air, looking out to the horizon, and let out a loud whinny.

"Easy, boy," Issie reassured him. "He'll be back. You'll see him again soon."

She gave Nightstorm a firm pat on his glossy bay neck. It was hard to believe that tomorrow, after more than a month in Spain, she would finally be taking her horse back to Chevalier Point.

Once the stallion was home, then the real adventure would begin. After all, they had come here to reclaim Storm so that Issie could train him to compete as her international eventing horse. Although, with everything that had happened since they arrived, Issie wondered whether their plans might have changed. But she needn't have been concerned.

"Storm is everything I had hoped he would become and more," Avery reassured her. "This horse is destined for greatness, Issie. He's going to be an international

221

eventer and you're going to be on his back all the way to the top."

They were going home. And they were preparing for a new, even more exciting journey. This time, it was serious.

This time, they were taking on the world.

PONY CLUB SECRETS

Liberty
and the
Dream Ride

Stacy Gregg

Issie is competing on the international circuit against
the best riders in the world!

But she must make tough choices if she's going to turn
the dream ride into a reality…

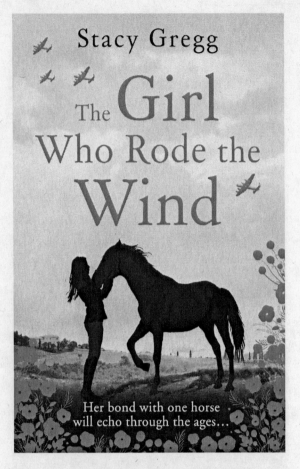

Stacy Gregg

The Girl
Who Rode the
Wind

Her bond with one horse
will echo through the ages...

An epic, emotional story of two girls and their bond
with beloved horses, the action sweeping between Italy
during the Second World War and the present day.

One family's history of adventure and heartbreak –
and how it is tied to the world's most dangerous
horse race, the Palio.

Printed by RR Donnelley at Glasgow, UK